The STOLEN
MANUSCRIPT

A MYSTERY IN THE **TIM TENDER** SERIES

R AY E . S PENCER

Archway Publishing books may be ordered through booksellers or by contacting:

Archway Publishing
1663 Liberty Drive
Bloomington, IN 47403
www.archwaypublishing.com
844-669-3957

Because of the dynamic nature of the Internet, any web addresses or links contained in this book may have changed since publication and may no longer be valid. The views expressed in this work are solely those of the author and do not necessarily reflect the views of the publisher, and the publisher hereby disclaims any responsibility for them.

This is a work of fiction. All of the characters, names, incidents, organizations, and dialogue in this novel are either the products of the author's imagination or are used fictitiously.

Any people depicted in stock imagery provided by Getty Images are models, and such images are being used for illustrative purposes only. Certain stock imagery © Getty Images.

ISBN: 978-1-6657-2523-1 (sc)
ISBN: 978-1-6657-2522-4 (hc)
ISBN: 978-1-6657-2524-8 (e)

Library of Congress Control Number: 2022911136

Print information available on the last page.

Archway Publishing rev. date: 06/21/2022

PROLOGUE

Tim Tender was hired to resolve the disappearance and, later, murder of a notable author in the case of the stolen manuscript.

He had learned some of his skills as a private investigator as far back as the days when he had grown up in a small, west-central town in Florida, called Saint Petersburg. At the time, he had been a student at Lakeside Elementary in his sixth-grade, big-shot year. He was instrumental, along with his twin brother, Todd; his two best friends, Link and Dink Playlen (also twins but physical duplicates); and the fifth-grade teacher at the school, Annie Tester, earlier a graduate of her namesake's Annie Oakley Fast-Draw Institute, in solving the killings of Jewish and Polish residents who had been living in the community. The evildoers were a crazed ex-Nazi adjunct commandant, who had become the principal of Lakeside, and his seriously brainwashed secretary who later became his wife. After advice from Tender and Miss Tester, the local school board vowed this situation would never happen again. They had promised the local citizens of St. Petersburg, after the awful atrocities that had taken place in their town, to do a thorough job in checking the backgrounds of people applying for city positions. Tender felt that he developed a knack and a love for solving things in those early days, which was why in college, he decided to study crime and how to unravel mysteries.

After reading the remarkable book *The Big Sleep* by the marvelous writer of detective fiction Raymond Chandler, Tender knew that PI was the title he eventually wanted next to his monogram. Being privately employed and not a wage earner of the city was one thing he desired. The feeling had hit him as hard as when Floyd Patterson KO'd Archie Moore, a fighter exactly twice Floyd's age, in round five at Chicago, November 30, 1956. That event took place after the great Rocky Marciano had retired the same year with an amazing record of 49–0.

Philip Marlowe, the mythical private eye in Chandler's novels, along with the great Sam Spade, dreamt up by another fabulous penman of the hard-boiled story, Dashiell Hammett, became posters on the walls of Tender's young life, presiding in prominence on the plaster next to two of his horror favorites, Fredric March and Vincent Price. The whole family of banners now adorned the walls of his one-man, one-woman office in the state of the famed Orioles. Since arriving in Baltimore, Tender had lived and worked within a once-sleepy city in Maryland—Laurel, a suburb between Baltimore and Washington, DC, off the BW Parkway. It was much like his hometown in Florida, where people seemed to prefer *laid-back*, a term that *slow* covered during the fifties in Tender's Saint Petersburg.

But, now, the dead body of a famous resident who had lived on Silverbirch Lane in the exclusive Montpelier section of Laurel had turned up. What made it a high-profile case was that the corpse was the best-selling writer of horror classics, Jake Venom. Tim found it a little ironic that a book and a flick that the writer had created contained the *Tender* label as part of their titles.

The movie, *Tender Nightmare*—hailed by the cinema-going public as scarier than Hitchcock's *Psycho*, released in 1960, at the beginning of the hippie decade—was pulling in box office receipts previously unheard of. Jake had written the screenplay, which was based on "his" publication by the same title; the book had been his latest release, retailing five million copies, far outdistancing his prior prize winner, *The Ghost of Auguste Escoffier Tours the Carlton,* which sold just five hundred thousand books. *Tender Nightmare*, the novel, had been Venom's only success in the last five years. His publishing house had marketed a weak effort, *The Fascist Dean*, four years back, and it had bombed at the bookstores. His latest, supposed comeback story, *The Godfather of Bane*, never reached Jake's editor at Premature Burial Publishing. He was killed on the way to the post office. The manuscript turned up missing.

Venom was seemingly done in, execution-style, with a bullet square between the eyes. His body was discovered behind the dumpster of an office building north of the Inner Harbor area downtown. The circumstances surrounding the death weren't as obvious as they appeared. What was found hanging from his right wrist and the items stuffed into his mouth constituted some real oddities in the cop's discovery of Venom's corpse, evident in the first chapter of this story.

Tim Tender was good at his craft; he had solved difficult cases, even as young as his business was, which was the reason Mrs. Venom, Vicki, had decided to employ the Tender PI Company. Although PI Tender didn't proceed in the same aggressive, tough manner as the fictional private detectives Marlowe and Spade, he was as determined to find justice as they were. He had inherited the easygoing style of his father, which made Pop a top-notch car salesman at Grant Ford on their native-born soil. Tender found that it also made things easier with the cops he dealt with consistently.

People didn't need to be fooled by Tender's unassuming modus operandi. He was wiry, but it was six feet of solid wire, and he had taken involuntary boxing lessons at his high school, Lakehood Senior, so he could put his foot down if necessary. Also, from his Florida beach days, he had inherited a constant tan and looked like a tall pretzel stick.

His partner's handle was Bea E. Hopkins, a beautiful, competent, confident woman. She was a former Lakehood High star softball player who also had lived in Saint Petersburg but was originally from Baltimore. Tender and Bea were engaged to be married and were a good team. When they stood face-to-face, he could kiss the top of her head. When he did so, he would always smell her hair, which was dark and straight and fell beyond her shoulder blades.

Bea's dream had always been to play for one of the professional women's baseball teams that performed during some of the years of World War II, like her twin idols, Eilaine and Ilaine Roth, who held down the up-the-middle positions, second base and shortstop, for the Muskegon Lassies. Bea had been a first basewoman. Unfortunately, the league disbanded in 1954, but she had no regrets.

She had finished her formal education several years before her fiancé. Bea had transferred to Patterson High on Kane Street in Baltimore after she had an awful experience in the Florida town with a not-so-capable, now deceased clairvoyant. But that's a tale for another time.

Tender had studied criminal law at a university in a town north of Los Angeles and began his investigating career in the City of Angels. Tender minored in psychology in California.

During the year that the master storyteller of terror, Jake Venom, was killed, the average human life expectancy was 71.1 years.

Unfortunately, the cessation of foul play did not end with Jake Venom's well-attended, star-studded, dual cremation ceremonies: the first one at the Baltimore gravesite of the legendary author, Edgar Allan Poe, Venom's hero, and the second one at the one-time Maryland residence of the writer and poet. Poe was the creator of one of Tender's favorites, "The Fall of the House of Usher."

CHAPTER 1

"Hey, Rip, that Jake Venom, huh?" Tender asked his plainclothesman friend, a man who looked like a drill sergeant: wide, muscular shoulders; short-cropped, silver-blond hair; and a square jaw. The police detective reminded Tender of his brother, his twin in mischievous crime in the past, Todd. Ripken Omaha was a durable cop; discounting days off and vacation periods, he hadn't missed a day on the beat for 2,131 days in a row. He even had his nose busted by a DUI collar in his early days on traffic cop duty—and still showed for work the next day. Omaha had broken another policeman's record for consecutive keeping-the-peace days: a man who had been a foot soldier in New York City, home of the dreaded Yankees, Officer Louis Henry, who had previously held the record of 2,130 between the years of 1925 and 1939. They were astonishing accomplishments in both cases. The lieutenant presently worked out of Central District 1, which covered urban areas like the Inner Harbor, the Theatre District, the adult schoolyard section called "the Block," district houses of government, and many hotels and residences. The sector of Baltimore also drew millions of tourists each year, which made law enforcement even more difficult.

"That's him, PI—Mrs. Venom hire you?"

"Yes, after her husband turned up missing. Said he was going to mail a manuscript and then head to the Freedom Inn for some crab cake sandwiches, but he didn't come home. Kind of peculiar that he left on Monday, but she didn't call me until Wednesday." Tender held back at present information about the story being lost.

"Hey, the Freedom uses the most lump and backfin meat, the firmest lett—"

"Yes, I know. I've heard it all before."

Even though the cop/private eye relationship was one that traditionally didn't flourish, Lt. Omaha and PI Tender had started associating with each other when they'd realized that they had something in common: both their first wives had left them.

Omaha's worse half had run off with Kal Kasner, a Hollywood type, who directed and acted in three-hour epic films. Kasner had told Omaha's wife that she had a wonderful singing voice, and he could make her a star of musicals. He told her that with the success of *Hair*, which started off-Broadway in 1967, the art form was making a comeback.

In Tender's breakup, the situation was much better than his cop crony's. Tim and his former spouse had decided to go their separate ways and remain friends for the sake of their son, Tim Jr.; Mom and son still lived in Saint Petersburg, but Tender Sr. loved his kid, and they interacted regularly. Tender knew that his ex-wife was a wonderful mother. Unfortunately, she couldn't exist with the "worst" of his bad habits.

Omaha, acting on counsel from Tender about what Raymond Chandler had once quoted—"A really good detective never gets married"—decided that he would never take the fall again. Of course, Omaha had always asked Tender why he hadn't followed the writer's suggestion in his own life. Tender said it was only Chandler's opinion, and now he had found the woman he wanted to spend the rest of his days with, Bea, his equal half.

Tender nodded in the direction of the dead Venom. "What's on his right arm?"

"Believe it or not, it's a Webster's Dictionary. Here, use my pen to flip through these page numbers on this log. Be careful—it's a Paper Mate. Here's a pad; write down the words that are highlighted." Tender knew that Omaha didn't want his chum to corrupt any evidence at the crime scene.

Tender bent down and crossed under the yellow-and-black tape surrounding the crime scene. "I have my own notebook and pen, a Montblanc."

"Well, excuse me for livin', hon!" Omaha said with a smile.

"What's with the 'Caution: Wet Paint' on the strip surrounding the body?"

"All the 'Police Line: Do Not Cross' ones are being used; Captain Calvert ordered more, but Chief Crossland said they haven't arrived."

"Busy day, huh?"

"It's Thursday in Baltimore."

The phrase that Tender came up with after flipping through the dictionary pages was, "A bad boy deserved it was were you." Tender scratched his chin. "What is that supposed to mean? Do we label it the 'Bad Grammar Killer Case'?"

"Shuffle the words." Omaha used a lot of poker and billiard terms when he spoke. Not Omaha Hold'Em—an obvious choice—but Seven Stud was his favorite card game; he usually won at it. But Tender almost always beat him at billiards; he preferred to play straight pool, a game where luck didn't enter the game.

"You were a bad boy; it was deserved," PI Tender stated. "Revenge murder, huh? Any prints on the book?"

"No, lab boys dusted. He's got a slug between his eyes; looks like it could've been a hit. Small cannon shot just like the round ricocheted directly off the eight ball."

"Think he was on the take with the mob?" Tender questioned.

"Wouldn't have thought it, but his nose area does look somewhat raw. Get a little closer, check out his mouth."

"It's full of oysters!"

"Definitely a full house," Omaha said.

"Are those bloodstains on his shirt?"

"Cocktail sauce. Sergeant Small was able to get a little taste. Negligible amount of blood around the wound; the coroner's boys will handle the scene. I'll check with ballistics later to find out about the *pistola*, and with the M.E. to see if his death was caused by the tiny torpedo lodged in his head. I'm hungry; how 'bout Costa's Restaurant for some crabs and a ginger beer?"

Off duty, Tender occasionally liked a Beefeater and soda but could only drink it with ice and the juice of a chunk of lime squeezed into the mix. He never drank more than one at a time. Bea, his beloved, liked a glass of dry red wine, cabernet sauvignon especially, but lately it had been giving her headaches, so she had switched to an arid white, chardonnay, preferring the grape of the French vineyards to those of the Napa Valley.

"Let's take my ride. I'll drop you off later to get yours," the cop told the gumshoe. Omaha drove a 1958 Ford Edsel—three-tone job, different shades the same color as champagne. His was from the Citation series. Tender learned from Omaha that he wanted horsepower and tailfins. The car seller had stated to Omaha that the Edsel would be "big"—a luxury model that would compete against the great ones from Buick and Oldsmobile, and even the New Yorker from Chrysler. As popular as the car was supposed to become, the police detective felt he could get a newer model every three years and get a good trade-in value to boot.

"Told you this baby would be worth some money—you know I'm a charter member of the Edsel Owner's Club, signed on in '69. My purchase price will be increased as if I caught my fourth ace in Five-Card Draw.

"I say bye-bye, good investment," Tender said. "Now, talk about an instant legend: my 1965 Mustang, 289 powerhouse, could blow out your doors."

"That's *in*, not *out*. You're as dumb as a scratched cue ball."

"Minor detail, huh. The original 'stang in '64, by its first birthday on April 17, 1965, sold over four hundred thousand cars, about four times the total Edsels that were made in the first twenty-five months on the market." Tender's vehicle was black with a white convertible top; Dad Tender had put a generous down payment on it for him, as a graduation present, after his youngest twin completed his criminal justice degree at Fresno State in California.

Classic cars were another reason the two justice seekers got along famously.

Tender said, "Yes, Costa's sounds great. I can play some keno."

CHAPTER 2

The Monday Before, 5:00 p.m. EST

Morris Mechanix was driving his bright red limousine—a converted half-ton 1959 GMC panel truck with its original chrome grill, shiny bumpers, and flashy fenders—to the Lord Baltimore Hotel, downtown. He was picking up a group of high rollers who wanted to check out the boardwalk and Steel Pier in Atlantic City as a possible place to build some casinos and introduce gambling. He had serviced the group before, as they had been to the home of the Colts and Orioles several times in the past. Once, he'd taken them to Pimlico for the Preakness, and he knew that they were very generous. The Baltimore metropolitan hotel was also home to Mechanix's tiny, one-man-answering-service transportation business. He mostly serviced the Baltimore–Washington International Airport but would also run private charters.

His vehicle still had the prototype radio, heater, cigar lighter, clock, and seat covers, which were all options at the time of production. Later, at his selection, he had an eight-track tape deck installed and added seats in the back-loading area of the vehicle, yielding spaces, along with the front passenger bench, for six persons not including himself. There would be three this run. The only inconvenience was that the clients had to enter from the rear double doors of the van. But because windows were not a part of the back portion of the cab, vices could be perfected on the way to destinations, a feature much appreciated by many of his clients.

Mechanix was running late; the reservation was for 5:30 p.m., and he was stuck in rush hour traffic on the Baltimore–Washington Parkway. He had always prided himself in meeting his patrons on time—especially big spenders like the ones he was transporting on today's trip. They wanted things to click, with no hang-ups, and a good portion of Mechanix's money came from tips.

He was stuck behind an old Edsel the color of Dom Perignon that was in the fast lane going about twenty-five miles per hour. Mechanix got extremely impatient and laid on the horn. The other car finally moved into the slow lane, and Mechanix gave the other driver the finger as he zoomed by the slowpoke. It took him over five minutes to get around the vehicle. Mechanix screamed, "Go back to the rest home, you relic!"

Mechanix was dressed in an all-white uniform with a patch sewed on the shirt that read, "Mechanix's Limo Service." He wore a royal blue ball cap—with the same logo—that hid his young gray hair. His body shape and uniform made him look somewhat like a burly Pillsbury Dough Boy. His azure eyeballs completed the Poppin' Fresh look.

The hand-painted signs that decorated each door of his truck-style taxi flashed the same business title with a phone number, but it also displayed the phrase, "No rush, no fuss, we get you there on time with old-time efficiency!" With such an advertisement, Mechanix couldn't afford to be tardy. He didn't even have time to look in his map book for the most efficient route to take to the New Jersey city on the shore. He hated to be ill-prepared—drove him nuts.

Besides, he wasn't in a good mood; earlier in the day, he had picked up some passengers—a half dozen coed suits—with the Yellow Condiment Marketing Group and dropped them off at Northwest Airlines. They had been to the Laurel Park Racetrack. Mechanix gave them plenty of time to make their flights. All they could come up with between them was a dollar in change, less than seventeen cents apiece, and a small jar of mustard. They offered him some excuse about losing all their paper on the ponies. The limo driver didn't buy it. Mechanix was good with numbers and could break them down as fast as Jim Palmer, a pitcher for the professional baseball team in Crabville, could hum the pellet to home plate at Memorial Stadium.

Mechanix halted his unique limousine in front of the hotel on West Baltimore Street at 5:45 p.m., fifteen minutes beyond pickup time. He mumbled to himself about wanting to nail that turtle on the Parkway.

"Good afternoon, Mr. Linguine," Mechanix said as the door to room 1939 pulled back. The Sicilians spoke good English except for the eldest, who spoke only Italian and didn't speak to anyone but his associates.

Linguine, being born in the "New Country" and not the "Old One," vocalized without any discernable Italian accent. He was also UCLA-educated. "Where have you been, paisano?"

"Scusi, got stuck in rush hour traffic, behind a slow driver."

"Scusi, that's good. Hey, Pasta, he got stuck in traffic."

"His name is Pasta?" Mechanix said.

"That's right, we've never told you his first name. Pasta E. Fagioli."

"A likely excuse," Pasta said. Fagioli was from Palermo, like the eldest Sicilian, but also spoke passable English.

"Don't worry, we just got back ourselves—from the Bay and Surf Restaurant in Laurel. Couldn't even get any calamari, manicotti, or stuffed shells," Linguine said.

"Yes, had to settle for the waiter's choice of cream of crab soup and crab imperial," Fagioli chimed in.

"Yes, that's tough to take," Mechanix replied. He could've told them that Little Italy, where they prepare marvelous Italian fare in many restaurants, was just around the bend from the hotel, but he knew that making customers feel foolish in any way might cause their hands to drop deeper into their financial pockets and remain buried there.

"They banned us from the restaurant—complained a little too much, I guess. We would never have returned anyway unless they changed the menu. Get Don Vermicelli, and let's go," Linguine commanded. "I've been acting as the leader since the don became ill after smoking too many Italian cigarettes and drinking too much caffe coretto."

"Caffe coretto?"

"Coffee corrected with a shot of cognac—in his case, always a double."

"Is he going to be all right for the trip? It's not exactly down the road, you know," the driver wondered.

"He's okay. He wants to go back to Sicily to die, but he's not ready just yet. Perhaps you can help us with some airline tickets later in that regard. But first, others to Los Angeles."

"Absolutely. Why LA?"

"He says that Mario Puzo stole his life story for the novelist's book, *The Godfather*, and called him Don Corleone when it should have been Don Vermicelli. He wants to set the record straight. From an acquaintance, we were pointed toward a Vincent March in Los Angeles—at Premature Burial Publishing Company. Also, I would like to take my colleagues to some places that I used to enjoy when at UCLA."

"How, per favore?"

"You've picked up some Italian phrases. Nice touch. We'll discuss it on the Atlantic City trip."

Linguine was dressed in navy blue Armani from head to toe and had dark, wavy hair and lots of gold and diamonds—a young stallion on the rise. He was a *caporegime* (lieutenant) but also acted as *consigliere* (counselor) to the don. His first name was Aldo.

Fagioli looked like an oak tree trunk with lanky legs dressed in a brown leisure suit and brown gloves—not the typical "mafioso" look, but he wanted to keep up with the times. He didn't have a chance to finish high school in his native country. His father had been rubbed out, and the teenage Pasta had to drop out and start his mob duties early to support the remaining members of the family: his mother, a nine-year-old sister, and an infant brother.

He had lost his right ear in his rookie year as a hitman: the target had wrestled away Pasta's switchblade long enough to slice off the acoustic organ, already vegetable-shaped, but Pasta recovered to complete the contract.

Fagioli was a devoted soldier to his don, and Don Jonah Vermicelli was dressed all in black: black pants, black shirt, black tie, black patent leather shoes, black socks, black fedora, and black jacket with wide lapels and padded shoulders, like the top part of the famed zoot suit of the 1940s. The don also walked in a bent-over manner, slowly. He had liver spots covering most of his face, and probably his hands too, but they couldn't be seen because of the black gloves that he constantly wore. He was thin like a worm but was still the boss; there was no question. But he was old and sick, so Linguine made most of the decisions, with Jonah's blessing. Vermicelli's mother had named him Jonah because she had always loved the story in the Bible of Jonah and the whale. Unfortunately, her Jonah didn't quite choose the path in life that she wanted him to go down: that of a Roman Catholic priest.

The trio of mobsters and their chauffeur left the Lord Baltimore and motored toward the boardwalk on the Atlantic Ocean. The three had their black stretch, a Lincoln Continental, which Fagioli usually operated, but he was weary from the Laurel roundtrip.

Mechanix hoped he could remember the best route to take; he didn't want his customers to think that he didn't know where he was going or what he was doing.

CHAPTER 3

Wednesday, 2:00 p.m. EST
The Day Before Jake Venom Passed

PI Tender stopped his classic Mustang in front of the two-story house on Silverbirch that was white with green trim. It was the home of celebrated author Jake Venom. Tender's radio was belting out "Dippermouth Blues" by Louis Armstrong, the great trumpeter and singer from the home of Mardi Gras, a carnival that Tender one day hoped to attend.

Vicki Venom, Jake's wife, had been given a recommendation from her husband's publisher in LA, the owner of Premature Burial Publishing, who had heard that Tender's agency was successful at solving complex cases in the City of Angels, so she contacted the Tender PI Company when her famous spouse vanished the Monday of that week.

Mrs. Venom answered the door somewhat sparsely dressed, and Tender noticed her body was perfect but didn't match her late-fifties face. It was as if she had run out of money when the cosmetic surgeon started to carve on her mug; there was a bit of sag. She invited Tender into the living room, which was to the left of the honey maple front door. A fire was blazing in the brick fireplace in the bowels of the east wall. The room was full of trophies, awards, and pictures of Jake Venom chummy with other people, mostly celebrities. Before moving from the foyer into the living chamber, Tender observed stairs leading to the second floor with a restroom at the top, and a hallway to the right of the stairs that led to a family room, where orioles—female Bullock's, Tender thought—were feeding just outside a pair of sliding glass doors.

"Good afternoon, Mr. Tender." Mrs. Venom saw him staring at the birds. "Oh, yes, Jake usually feeds the birds, but I had to today—he said they like berries, so I threw them some junipers."

"Afternoon, Mrs. Venom." Tender noticed that the feathered ones seemed to be wobbling somewhat. "You do realize that gin is made from juniper berries?"

"No, I did not know that fact. Do you think they are drunk?

"Possibly. It's my job to be nosy; I was wondering, considering the initial of your last name is *V*, why is there an *M* on your garage?"

"My husband had that put on there on my birthday after we first moved in. My nickname is Monetary."

"How nice, huh."

"Mr. Vincent March approved your services; he's the head of my husband's publishing firm in Los Angeles. He had heard of your agency and said to contact you. He used to own an office here in Baltimore. Mr. March just had his seventieth birthday and is still steering the ship, amazing. He's an author too; wrote a book called *Five Easy Steps to Publishing a Book.*"

Tender thought, *Number one: Buy or inherit your own publishing company.* "He approved my services?"

"Oh, yes. I never do anything without checking with Jake, but he's not here; Mr. March was the next best thing, a friend. Can I light you a Camel? Do you mind if I smoke?"

"Well, it's your house. Thanks, no; never touch 'em. So, what can I help you with, huh?"

"Mr. Tender, my husband left here on Monday to mail his latest manuscript to Los Angeles and still hasn't returned. He left me a note. I was at the hairdresser most of the day getting the treatment:

massage, mud bath, manicure and pedicure, and the new Pat Nixon bouffant. Theo, my savior, performed magic—the Mane Magician. Do you like it?"

"Very regal! What salon?"

"The Milhous Salon on Pennsylvania Avenue, in DC."

"I'll have to tell my fiancée; she'd love that style. What did the note say that your husband left you?"

"The note said that after he sent the story, he was going down to the Freedom Inn on Erdman to pick us up a couple of crab cake sandwiches. Theirs are the best because they use the most lump and backfin meat, firmest lettuce, juiciest tomatoes, and Hellmann's— real mayonnaise, not that salad dressing stuff. I know Freedom Shopping Center is a pretty good way from here, but I didn't think it would take two days."

"What about tartar sauce?"

"Oh, heavens no! Don't blaspheme."

"Sorry."

"Jake began sending his manuscripts after he had fired his agent sometime before *Tender Nightmare* came out."

"Why did he fire his agent?"

"Excuse me, Mr. Tender. I hear the phone ringing."

PI Tender started scanning the photographs that were on the mantel above the brick furnace. There was one with James Michener and Jake Venom holding tall glasses with umbrellas sticking out of the top, toasting something with the drinks—mai tais, Tender guessed. A lei was around each author's neck. Another picture showed the fright writer standing in the middle of the two great Baltimore ballplayers, the Robinsons, Brooks and Frank, the American League MVPs in 1964 and 1966, respectively. Tender immediately thought about his all-time favorite player, Mickey Mantle, who had held the same title on three different occasions. In the picture, which was somewhat fuzzy, the three notables were standing beside an old panel truck, painted a brilliant red and with some sort of writing on the front door. Because of the dimness and the way the three men were standing, Tender couldn't quite make out the phrase; only the words "on time" were clear enough to decipher. Venom's house was in the background of the photo.

Mrs. Venom came back into the room with a huge grin on her face. "Sorry about the interruption, Mr. Tender."

"Who was on the phone?"

"Oh, just some kids who wanted to know if I had Prince Albert in a can. I said, 'Of course, it's the brand of pipe tobacco my husband smokes,' and they sa—"

"I know. 'You'd better let him out.' Hilarious."

"Kids these days," Mrs. Venom said with a chuckle.

"So why did your husband fire his agent?"

"I'm not sure. Some disagreement. He never really discusses his business affairs with me. When he writes, he always keeps the doors to his office shut. Says he needs complete silence—although he sneezes a lot when he's creating. Jake sometimes sends me memos under the door. Even yelled at me on paper. I don't like that."

"A writer communicating through his writing. How apropos."

"Oh, Mr. Tender, you speak Italian?"

"Right. Can I see his office, huh?"

"Oh, no, he never lets anyone go in there, not even me; I would like to get in there someday to clean. Maybe when you locate him, he'll let you in?"

"You don't seem all that upset that he's missing."

"Well, he sometimes disappears for days at a time, not telling me where he's going, but with the note, I thought I'd better call you."

Tender didn't push that situation any further, at least not now. He prepared to leave the house, promising Vicki Venom to contact her if he came up with anything about the two-day crustacean brunch run. He knew that he had to get into the office later, somehow.

As an afterthought, Mrs. Venom did mention that Jake drove a multi-coated, emerald green, '68 XJ 6 Jaguar, which was gone from the two-car garage. But she also said his keys were still on the hook hidden behind the framed dollar bill, the first buck he had made from *Tender Nightmare*, his biggest seller. She sloughed it off and said he probably had an extra set ground and had failed to mention it. Tender thought it curious.

Also, she noted that his trench coat, the only warming apparel he would wear, was still hanging in the hall closet. An odd occurrence, Tender felt, with the climate being as glacial as it had been that week.

Tender was off to the Freedom Inn, where, because of Venom's celebrated face, seventy-five-inch-tall frame, and striking white haircut Beatles style, closest to Lennon's, someone might have remembered seeing Jake.

Before exiting, Tender garnered a check from Mrs. Venom for his fee for a week. If it took less than seven days to finish the job, they would settle the difference later; also, expenses would be figured at that time.

CHAPTER 4

Thursday, 5:00 p.m. EST
The Day of Jake Venom's Death

As the bubbly-colored Edsel was traveling up North Point Road toward Costa's, Omaha told Tender a juicy tidbit about the Krueger suds. Omaha had this thing about firsts. "Hey, PI, did you know that Krueger beer was the first beer to be canned?"

"No, I didn't. Huh." All Tender was interested in now was getting to Costa's and watching the Keno board bounce up the digits in the bar. The restaurant hailed to have some of the best hard-shell blue crabs in the state of Maryland—usually using only the better-tasting, large males—had a large dining room on one side of the building and a cozy lounge on the other. Tender had never even seen the dining half. The kitchen was between the two rooms, and food was served on either side. "Order me an orange soda, will ya? I'm going to put some numbers down."

Tender usually played the same six digits on his Keno ticket: 5, 9, 43, 12, 26, and 39, which were a combination of his and Bea's birthdates. Sometimes he would wager a Super 20 Spot Special, choosing the maximum amount of numbers, hoping to hit the big one, a jackpot of one hundred thousand dollars. He hadn't accomplished that yet, but he was persistent. The pastime, as Tender called it, always put him in the gray area between the excitement of winning and the fear of losing. He rejoined his buddy at their table. As each number came up on the board, Tender squirmed in his seat.

"You realize, Rip, that Keno was originated in China by Cheung Heung over two thousand years ago to raise capital for his province's diminishing army. From what I have read, it was prosperous. It's done all right by me. They called it the Chinese lottery." Tender knew a lot about the history of gambling. Possibly that was not such a good thing.

"Yeah, right."

While the PI was putting his money down, the waitress had dropped a dozen beer-steamed crabs—smothered with the wonderful Old Bay seasoning—on the old *Baltimore Sun* newspapers that covered the table. Omaha had already malleted deep into his initial, colossal claw. Because he hailed from Havre de Grace, Maryland, Ripken Omaha knew the dismantling, cracking, and picking process like the back of his hand. Tender learned the method from him at their original sit-down lump crap feast; the novice had asked for melted butter and a lobster cracker with his hard-shell blues.

"So, PI, do you think the words emphasized in the dictionary were meant to be a clue to the cops, or just to let Venom know that he screwed up somehow?"

"I think both. I believe the killer is the type who gets great joy out of revenge but also wants a good chase. Otherwise, he could have simply told Jake to his face that he had messed up—possibly add a little torture to the formula. Or maybe he was just using the dictionary so his handwriting couldn't be analyzed."

"Good point. You don't think it was possibly an execution by La Cosa Nostra for some gambling debts or coke payments missed, or some other indiscretion to the wrong people?"

"Sicilian rubout? Could be. Guess we're going to have to do some further investigating into the horror king's background, huh?"

"Works out pretty good, the way we assist each other," Lieutenant Omaha said.

They finished up the rest of the crabs a half-hour later.

"I need to get back to the office. I'll catch you later. Let me know what you find out downtown," PI Tender said.

"How are you going to get there? I drove you, remember?"

"Right—uh, yeah, I'll ring a cab. The crime scene is a little out of the way from the station house. Save you some tread on your tires."

"You sure?"

"Go on. Don't worry 'bout me."

"I'll check with the M.E. and ballistics; hopefully, that will shed some light. Call you, PI."

"See ya, Rip."

After leaving the phone booth, Tender walked around to the back of the building and waited until his lunch chum was out of sight. Then the PI entered through the kitchen. He knew Chef Dyan on a first-name basis. Later, he would make a second trip to the telephone and, this time, he would call a taxi.

For now, there was more Keno to be played. But first, he had to wash his hands.

CHAPTER 5

Friday, 7:45 p.m. EST

Tender eyed the front of the three-tone red brick, three-story combination hotel and office building in which he worked and lived. The place was clean and inexpensive and had a certain old-world charm.

The front double doors were glass, trimmed in aluminum. There was a faded red carpet leading from the mirror-coated portals out to Churchfield Lane, and the rug was overshadowed by an awning with burgundy, blue, and white stripes that had four gray metal rods holding it in place. As he walked toward the door, he could see his reflection and the way his powder-blue tweed suit, dark blue shirt and tie, black wingtips, and thick black socks made him appear. PI Tender was the spitting image of PI Marlowe, except Tender didn't like to wear a fedora. Also, there was no bulge in his jacket; he didn't usually carry a gun. Tender always said, "I only use a gat when I smell a big rat." He did have a permit if he ever needed to conceal a weapon.

On the other side of the door, a dining room took up the whole left side of the bottom floor—good, cheap, wholesome food for breakfast, lunch, and dinner, and a burning-oil snack past midnight for the real late-nighters.

Straight back in the left corner was a check-in desk for the hotel, and directly across the thin hall, covered with the same, less-faded red carpet as outside, was the leasing office for the business suites. To the right, back toward the front of the structure, were stairs leading up to another hallway, this one much shorter. At the opposite end were the same number of steps stretching down to a tavern with a Maryland sports theme. It had posters of many famous jocks from Baltimore athletic teams: Johnny U, Lenny Moore, and Earl Morrall, all former NFL MVPs for the Colts; Frank, Brooks, and John "Boog" Powell, American League MVPs for the MLB Orioles; the NBA's 1968 and 1969 Rookies of the Year, respectively, Earl "The Pearl" Monroe and Wes Unseld; and a final picture that many people in Maryland would just as soon erase from their minds' eye: one that showed "Broadway" Joe Namath pointing his right forefinger toward the sky over Miami as he was jogging off the playing surface, indicating the New York Jets victory over the heavily favored Colts in Super Bowl III. It was left there as a harsh reminder. Tender watched most of his favorite sporting events in the charming environment of Baltimore athletics. Thankfully, there was no Keno board or any type of betting machinery.

Tender got off the elevator, took a short walk, and entered through the cherrywood doors of his office on the third floor of the brick edifice. On the glass, hand-painted on the left door was the phrase *Private Investigator*, and on the right was *Tim Tender*. The inside of the office could not be seen from outside in the hallway.

Bea Hopkins was not in the office; she was out shopping for slacks. She never liked to wear the same outfit twice in a row. "What woman would," was a sentiment Tender felt that Philip Marlowe would have expressed. Bea's philosophy on boutiques was, "If it's on sale, buy it." She always said, "Otherwise, someone else will get the money I'm supposed to rescue!"

Tender walked to his honey maple desk and sat down in a swivel chair. The desk had a red telephone, a green blotter, and a black Sam Spade pen and holder set. The working bureau also held a very unique paperweight: a glass one that enclosed a rather large booger, made for Tender by his four-minute-older twin and coach, Todd, as a part of his twelve-step program to keep the nasty-picking habit under control—to the present day, a resounding success for the younger brother.

Behind the wooden furnishing were three flags spaced exactly one foot apart: an American flag with a golden eagle perched on the flagpole's top, plus the state banners of Florida and Maryland. To the left of the flags were three, three-drawer file cabinets. All in all, it was a very colorful place.

Also, he had an old RCA record player that his sister, Kim, had given him, and he spun LPs on it when Bea was out. The other family members, Mom and Dad Tender, Rod, Todd, and Everett, Jr., had given Tender a bunch of oldies that he enjoyed immensely.

The red phone rang, and the shamus picked it up. "Private Investigator Tender here, may I help you?"

It was Lt. Omaha. "Got the word on Venom's cause of death: the bullet was a .22 short, only caliber to use rimfire. It didn't kill him, though. A lethal dose of snake venom found in his system, and some on his face, did him in—final hand played."

"Snake venom, huh? Trying to make some statement of symbolism, I presume, using the snake?" Tender said.

"Maybe. The chief M.E. said the juice came from a Sudanese spitting cobra and could have caused Jake to go temporarily blind from the amount on his mug. Plus, he said that cobra poison paralyzes the nerve center that controls heart behavior and breathing. He was typing up his toxicology report when I spoke to him."

"With the.22, I guess the killer wanted to make sure he was dead, huh? You locate the gun?"

"Or make it look like a hit? No, *pistola* is still missing. The M.E. also found cocaine in the body and said he thinks ole Jake was a pretty big coke user considering the extreme rawness under his nose."

"Overdose, huh?"

"No, not even enough for the ante, but maybe the killer knew Jake was heavy on the blow and enticed him with it," Omaha said.

"Maybe. Ballistics figure out what kind of gun, from the bullet?"

"Semiautomatic, Beretta Minx. Ballistics was Johnny-on-the-spot, too."

"Famous people get famous treatment," Tender said. "What about prints?"

"Yeah, turns out that Mr. Venom, horror writer supreme, was a friend of the district attorney. No, no prints are evident."

"Gloves, most likely, huh? Mrs. Venom identify the body?"

"Yeah; she left about an hour ago."

"Is she a suspect?"

"Not presently. Her whereabouts are confirmed by Theo, the hairdresser—or should I say the Mane Magician, as his business card states."

"As Mrs. Venom had referred to him?"

"Right. Mrs. Venom seemed to be in a hurry and wasn't here when the coroner's office discovered the cobra milk. Gotta go. Oh, by the way, M.E. said he thought the body had been there about three days, Jake's chips probably cashed in sometime on Monday, late morning or early afternoon. See ya, PI."

"Talk to you later, Rip. Thanks."

As soon as he hung up with Lt. Omaha, the phone rang again.

"I've been trying to call; the phone was busy," Bea E. Hopkins said.

"I've been talking to Rip," Tender said.

"What about?"

"You haven't heard?"

"Heard what?"

"Jake Venom—you know, the Jake Venom whom I've been looking for—turned up dead. The body was found downtown behind the dumpster of an office building."

"Is that on the square? That's terrible. How'd he die?"

"What did you say? 'Is that on the square'?"

"Sorry, I've just been reading Erle Stanley Gardner's *The Case of the Lonely Heiress*. It's good, and Della's so cool."

"Want me to save you some time and reveal the ending?"

"No!"

"Jake Venom had a slug in his head, between the eyes."

"Shot to death?"

"Shooting must've been a backup plan—poison from a snake was the actual cause of death, according to the M.E. It's a long, weird story; I'll fill you in later at the restaurant. Why don't you meet me there? From here, it'll take me forty-five minutes. Where are you, huh?"

"I'm at my aunt's place in Armistead Gardens. Late dinner, tonight, huh? Great, now you've got me saying that 'huh.' Where are we going?" Bea had moved in with her Aunt Beryl—her favorite—on East Federal Street when she had come from St. Petersburg. Bea had planned on getting her place when she got on her feet but now would simply wait until she and Tim got married and moved into their dream home. She hoped.

"How 'bout somewhere in Little Italy?"

"Sounds *delicioso*! Where in Litlitlee?"

"Chipparelli's on South High Street, all right? They have that great southern Italian."

"Yes, but you'd better give me directions; I'm not sure I remember how to get there from here. You know me: go east when I should go west, go north when it should be south, and versa vice. No, wait, reverse that—vice versa."

"Okay, get out your Montblanc." Even though he didn't hail from the "city of crabs," PI Tender knew the town well and would always give specific instructions. "From Federal, head west for two miles. Turn left on North Wolfe Street and then head south for one mile. You'll then be on South Wolfe Street; continue about six-tenths of a mile and turn right on Eastern Avenue, moving west for another six-tenths. Finally, turn right on South High, go one-tenth of a mile, and you'll be at Chipparelli's front door."

"Thanks, Timster, great directions." Bea liked to call him *Timster*, a cute pet name. Tender wasn't all that fond of it, but he felt it was no big deal. "I'm going to go now. See ya there."

"Why don't you wait about a half-hour? It should only take you 11.4 minutes because it's only 4.3 miles from your Aunt Beryl's, huh."

CHAPTER 6

Saturday, 8:00 a.m. EST

Mechanix's alarm was chiming; he knocked it off his dresser and onto the mahogany wood floor in his two-story row home in Armistead at the famed Gardens section of Baltimore. His place was situated directly in front of the Fox Mansion, a kind of large, local clubhouse for the community, where a board of directors decided who would receive their ninety-nine-year leases. Mechanix's stepfather owned the row home, which was listed in his name. Mechanix never knew his biological father, who took off and never returned to the family when the boy was a toddler. He was glad that his stepdad was taking care of his dear, sweet mother; they resided in Sanibel Island, Florida. He hadn't seen them for quite a spell.

The Fox Mansion was also home to teenage dance parties on Fridays and Saturdays, hiring a disc jockey to spin records. The soiree had lasted much longer than usual—late into the wee hours of that Saturday morning. Mechanix didn't get much sleep because the DJ kept his record machine cranked to its maximum volume.

Mechanix hadn't arrived home until after midnight on Friday, getting his Atlantic City trio back to the Lord Baltimore late.

Most of the trip was a disaster. The limo driver had gotten lost but did recover in enough time to keep tempers from flaring. It had rained much of the time, and Don Vermicelli had to stop and use the bathroom about a hundred times. Also, the downpour was so severe that Fagioli couldn't see any of the scenery or billboards. From the large signs, he was able to see, he sang a little tune—out of key—using whatever words were on the highway advertisements. Linguine, even though the weather hadn't cooperated, accepted Mechanix's assistance and garnered useful data for their future wagering ventures. Linguine was very grateful financially in Mechanix's direction.

Mechanix walked over to the small desk that faced the window that looked across to the Fox Mansion. There, he had his 1878 Remington typewriter, which had the shift key system with the upper and lower case on the same type bar, unlike the 1876 model. He had a thing for antiques and had purchased his machine for only $25 more than the original price of $125 for an 1874 Remington—it was a steal, Mechanix thought. And it worked wonderfully, except for one slight imperfection.

It was his passion to one day retire from the transportation business and become a full-time writer. He had already completed one full-length manuscript—a circumstance unfortunately connected to much writing sweat, proofreading sweat, and rewriting sweat for no reward. He was told by a so-called expert that his book was the worst story he had ever read. He had forgotten about the distressing incident and was now copying a second manuscript. He wrote under the pseudonym John Victor because he had lost some very good customers once. They had seen a magazine article he had written for *The Atlantic Monthly*, and they found another limousine firm, telling him that they believed Mechanix would soon disband his transfer agency for a communication career.

Click! Click! Click! The keys hit the paper—the only problem was none of what was reaching the modern form of parchment made any sense. Mechanix stopped and left his house. It was his day off, but he wasn't going to waste it. He grabbed some old tennis shoes because he didn't wear his Chuck Taylor All-Star Converse basketball sneakers anymore; they were signed by Chuck himself.

He had bought them because they were the official shoe of the Olympics since 1936, and they were discontinued after the 1968 games. Mechanix felt it was a very patriotic gesture and was sure the Taylors would become collectibles.

Mechanix put some food in the aquarium for his pets, where he had to move some old raw eggs; he made sure the lid was on tight. He straightened out his Grateful Dead and Quicksilver Messenger Service psychedelic posters reaped from forgotten days of the past. The concert advertisements decorated the wall right over a small table containing a strobe light. Mechanix had retrieved the Quicksilver masterpiece right off the chalkboard that announced coming attractions at Bill Graham's Fillmore Auditorium in San Francisco. Clever, he thought.

He reminisced for a moment; ran down the stairs; moved out the front door; and through the screened-in porch that he had built; he wasn't much with a hammer and nails or home improvement. He hopped into his vehicle, the same one that he used in his job. He usually kept his truck out back and covered with a canvas, but last night he had been too tired to make the attempt. He felt that cruising in his rig, even on his off day, was like driving a billboard around town, and he was sure that it helped increase his business. Besides, even though he had a substantial savings account balance at the Maryland National Bank, he couldn't afford another auto now. Inside his limo, he shoved in an eight-track tape, and the Beatles' "Lucy in the Sky with Diamonds" started to play. Mechanix immediately noticed the black-and-white Mustang convertible that he had to veer around to avoid hitting it, and he logged the moment in his mind. Without hesitation, Mechanix gave the other driver the bird and sped off. He was away to the Mason Travel Agency in Bowie, Maryland, to get information about airline tickets for the Sicilians, his top customers.

Tender slowly pulled up to Aunt Beryl's row home in Armistead Gardens. Bea had a pearly white that was suddenly killing her. Tender would drop her off at her dentist, Dr. Hugh Wunderman, who had agreed to an emergency visit, and then head over to Vicki Venom's house, hoping she would let him into Jake's office, considering Venom was dead and wasn't going to need the room any longer—with the possible exception of some ghostwriting.

Tender was still a little peeved at the imbecile who had almost hit him and fingered him out the driver's side window. It had happened so fast, and the other motorist had screeched off so quickly, that Tender had noticed only that the other vehicle was some type of older panel truck, red, and possibly a classic.

Tender didn't need to enter the unique row home. Bea rushed out holding her swollen mouth. The constant moaning caused Tender to put the pedal to the metal, but his version never surpassed the speed limit. Luckily, the dental complex was nearby on Edison Highway. One of Dr. Hugh's delightful and skillful hygienists, Mary or Holly, would take Bea home after the crisis molar treatment.

Tender dropped off Bea and retreated to snoop, a part of his self-imposed job description that he performed very well.

Mechanix was getting close to the toll booth before the Harbor Tunnel, and he fumbled for a token. He handed the toll taker his coin and some green paper and gave her a short wave. She ignored the gesture. He grumbled under his breath, "Yes, right, freak. You're too good to return courtesy to a lowly limo driver because your job is so damned important." He promised himself that the greeting would be the last speck of financial consideration he would show that money-grabbing creep.

Mechanix reached the travel agent's facility about fifty minutes after exiting the Harbor Tunnel, and he parked his truck just off Highway 50 in Bowie, Maryland. It was a much nicer drive on the weekends—not any business-week commuters dominating the roadways. He got the boarding passes to LA for his Sicilian customers on American Airlines, having his flight broker, Perry from Mason's Travel Agency, scan as many airlines as necessary to get the best price. And knowing his clients' propensity to stay at classic luxury hotels, he booked reservations at the Beverly Hills Hotel, which had originally opened on a hillside bordering Los Angeles in 1912.

He returned to his red limousine. He had a pit stop to make in Laurel before motoring toward the Lord Baltimore and a meeting with his favorite clients.

CHAPTER 7

Saturday 10:00 a.m. EST

Tender was again turning off the ignition to his Mustang in front of the two-story home in Montpelier, now solely owned by the widow of Jake Venom. He started up the walkway as a yellow taxi coasted in and parked behind his car. Vicki Venom came sprinting out faster than when the great Jackie Robinson, the NL MVP in 1949 for the Brooklyn Dodgers, swiped home.

"I'm sorry about your husband, Mrs. Venom. Are you going somewhere?"

"I'm flying out to Los Angeles to see Vincent. I need him to help me get through this. Probably be back right before the funerals. No decision made on the coroner's inquest yet; officials are too busy. I told Lieutenant Omaha everything I know; he said I could go but to keep in touch."

"What about me looking in Jake's office, huh?"

"I've changed my mind. I just can't allow that right now; it would be too emotional to enter the room. Maybe when I get back. Vincent will be waiting at LAX for my flight to arrive. Please find my husband's killer, as well as his latest manuscript, Mr. Tender. There will be a nice bonus in it for you. His ceremonies aren't until Thursday so that his good friend Lee Marvin can attend—Jake loved him in *Cat Ballou*. I'll most likely be here Wednesday." The cabbie opened the rear door for his passenger, and he drove her out of the neighborhood. She had left too quickly for Tender to gain any knowledge about her husband's true cause of death.

Curious, Tender thought. In their first meeting, Mrs. Venom referred to Jake's publisher only with "Mister" attached to his name, never just Vincent, as she had just done not once but twice. He shook it off and knew he had to get into the novelist's inner sanctum; he felt that there had to be some clue there that could help him shed sunlight on some possible secrets.

Tender waited until the amber taxi was completely out of sight. He put his gloves on; then, using some old tricks he had learned at an old house in his birthplace about how to gain access to secured buildings, he entered the horror king's ex-residence. The writer had taken the huge slumber, as Raymond Chandler might refer to it. Admission into the author's inner chamber was easier than when a housewife makes a homemade pie with a prebaked pie shell and canned fruit.

Once inside, Tender noticed that the desk and the chair behind it were both made of expensive white mahogany. The seat was a swivel type like the one in his own office, but this one came with leather and had been obtained in a furniture store much farther uptown than Tender's chosen chain outlet.

Tender was sitting in tanned-hide luxury, and he said out loud, "Man, a nice way to work, huh." He enjoyed the comfort as deep as the Grand Canyon when he saw a bookshelf, which was also carved out of the same wood as the other pieces of furnishing in the room and chock-full of literary first editions. Two tales that caught his eye were from a duo of fabulous British writers of gothic horror, *Dracula*, Bram Stoker's eerie yarn, and *Frankenstein*, the scary story of the put-together monster, penned by Mary Shelley.

He also recognized a copy of *The Norton Anthology of English Literature*, a book he had used many times in one of his elective classes at the college in California.

He walked over to the bookshelf and picked up the collection containing many superb writings ranging from the Middle Ages to the twentieth century. He took the cover carefully, with its depiction of the regally dressed Elizabeth I, between his right thumb and forefinger and flipped open the book. The title of the Anglo-Saxon epic poem *Beowulf* appeared. He had previously examined this piece allegedly composed by an Anglian poet of the eighth century, and he had enjoyed it immensely. He and his twin brother, Todd, had always read books like other people smoked cigarettes: one right after the other. He began to reacquaint himself with the Scandinavian culture hero and read aloud.

"Thus, these warriors lived in joy, blessed, until one began to do evil deeds, a hellish enemy. The grim spirit was called Grendel, known as the rover of the borders."

He put the book back, its shelf-life now, considering the death of its owner, probably doomed to one of not fulfilling its purpose to enlighten and entertain—blending Scandinavian history, pagan mythology, and conditions of Christianity.

Then, he saw another novel he was already familiar with: *Fahrenheit 451*, a book by Ray Bradbury, a courageous and visionary writer. Tender had read and much enjoyed his younger brother Eric's copy, signed by the author. It was a lesson on dystopia and on how to rid the Earth of knowledge through books, destroying them by fire at every opportunity.

Tender again began to indulge in hearing himself aloud, a method he sometimes used that made him feel somewhat like an actor in a play. He spoke from part 1, "The Hearth and the Salamander."

It Was a Pleasure to Burn

It was a special pleasure to see things eaten, to see things blackened and *changed*. With the brass nozzle in his fists, with this great python spitting its venomous kerosene upon the world, the blood pounded in his head, and his hands were the hands of some amazing conductor playing all the symphonies of blazing and burning to bring down the tatters and charcoal ruins of history.

Tender had to remain focused and return to the reason that he had entered the writer's room. Was he stretching the law in the name of justice? For a moment, he thought about what kind of half-man, half-fiend could have done the ultimate wicked deed to Jake Venom.

He sat back down and noticed a phone-number register—the metal type with pop-up letter sections. Tender tapped the button, flipped through the pages, and stopped at the *M*, eyeing a card sticking out. It was a business card, red with yellow lettering, stapled to the top of the page.

MM
Mechanix's Limo Service
Big Red Will Get You There "On Time"
With "Old-Time Efficiency"

Tender knew that there was something familiar about that slogan, but now he couldn't quite put his middle finger on it. He then began to flip back through the lettered pages and stopped when he saw the name "Cola" Bench, King. An address was listed in a somewhat legible scrawl. It was in the downtown section known as the Block, where there were strip joints, pornographic bookstores, pimp joints, and flophouse after flophouse standing as a tribute to the bottom side of life in Baltimore. Tender wondered what Jake Venom's connection to Sleezeville could be. Then it smacked him as solid as when Cassius Clay KO'd Sonny Liston in round 7 at Miami Beach on February 25, 1965. He spoke again to nobody: "Of course. *Cola* stands for *Coke*—cocaine; this guy must've been ole Jake's supplier." Tender wrote down the location on a piece of Venom's writing paper with a header logo that read, "The Deliverer of Deadly Dread."

Tender again surveyed the room with his baby browns and turned his focus toward the bottom of the desk. He saw there was a drawer with a padlock on it. Tender's picking talents were legendary, at least in his mind, and he handled the obstacle as easily as when Arthur Ashe defeated Tom Oker, in five sets, the first 14–12, in the men's singles at the US Open tennis tournament in 1968 at Forest Hills. This lock caused Tender some trouble, but he stuck with it, as Arthur had, and finally managed it.

What he found there was a rough draft of *Tender Nightmare* with a byline typed with just the initials, J. V. As he picked up the papers, a photo fell out onto the champagne-colored carpet. He retrieved it. The picture was an illustration of Jake and three men whom Tender didn't recognize, all standing in front of a black stretch limousine with a green, white, and red flag stuck to each front fender.

He began to peruse the rough draft. The first paragraph of the prologue, all in caps—in fact, scanning the manuscript, all the letters seemed to be capitalized—read.

THREE YEARS AFTER THE END QF QNE QF THE WQRST WARS IN THE HISTQRY QF THE WQRLD—A WAR THAT INVQLVED EACH QF THE EARTH'S MAJQR PQWERS—A NUMBER QF HAPPIER EVENTS TQQK PLACE.

With his keen eye for detail, the PI realized that all the *O*s were replaced with *Q*s. Was the typewriter that had been used defective? The typewriter in Venom's office, an Underwood, offered no clue; the *O* worked fine. But why would he write this story in such a manner? An odd occurrence, indeed.

Tender decided that he had retrieved enough data, knowing that he could come back in case something else struck him. His next step was to call upon a nasty part of downtown that he didn't care for but, in his job, had been forced to visit many times in the past.

As he was getting up from Venom's desk, he lifted his head and stared directly into the sunken eyes of a yellow ski mask. Then in the next instant, a blunt instrument pounded the top of his head, and Tender became one with his dreams.

CHAPTER 8

Saturday, 12:15 p.m. EST

Mechanix knocked on the door of room 1939.

There was no answer.

He heard the elevator door open and turned to observe Pasta E. Fagioli exiting, wearing another leisure suit, this one bright yellow.

"How ya doing, Mr. Fagioli?"

"Just fine."

"Where's Linguine and Don Vermicelli?"

"My don had to go to the restroom in the lobby—couldn't wait."

Mechanix thought that had he known about Fagioli's sunny outfit, he would have mentioned possibly needing his sunglasses. Instead, he stuck to his steadfast rule: no making fun of the customers.

In the next moment, the other two-thirds of Mechanix's clients came down the hallway.

"Sorry, but Don Vermicelli had—"

"Right, Mr. Linguine, I've already heard," Mechanix stated. "Where have you all been?"

"We drove our Lincoln Continental this morning and took it for a nice drive around the downtown and harbor areas. Did you get the tickets to LA and the hotel reservations?"

"Yes. Your flight, 4922, leaves at 2:40 p.m. from BWI and arrives at JFK at 3:50, where you'll have a thirty-five-minute layov—"

"I hate those layovers," Linguine stated.

"No direct flights available. Flight 117 departs New York at 4:25 and arrives in Los Angeles at 7:38," Mechanix said.

"That's only a three-hour flight from the Big Apple, Linguine. Not bad," Fagioli said.

"It's over a six-hour flight, several minutes over. The West Coast is three hours behind the East Coast," Mechanix informed them.

"It's okay. Fagioli doesn't understand time zone changes."

"Good thing there are no billboards in the clouds," Mechanix whispered to himself.

"What? I didn't understand you," Linguine said.

"Oh, nothing."

"Did you get chairs in first class?"

"Right. The first row of passenger seats, behind one of the galleys on the Baltimore–Washington to John F. Kennedy run."

"We need three chairs together!" Pasta said.

"Sorry, Mr. Fagioli, but there are only two seats on either side of the aisle in first class. That's the closest you can get. Unless you want to fly coach, where you can sit smack dab on top of each other. Also, back there you only get a snack instead of a fancy lunch or dinner."

"That's all right. We'll stay with the front. What kind of plane will we be on?" said Linguine.

"A Boeing 727-200, luxury jet. Only been in the air since 1968; I checked that out myself."

"Is there a restroom close for my don?"

"Yes, Mr. Fagioli, just beyond the front galley and right behind the cockpit. Mr. Vermicelli can say *ciao* to the pilot and copilot. I also booked you into a nice bungalow, number five, at the Beverly Hills Hotel on Sunset Boulevard. I think Howard Hughes may have stayed in that one on occasion—or was it, Liz Taylor? Oh, well. There are lots of sultry gardens and exotic floral areas for Mr.

Vermicelli to relax in, and Mr. Fagioli can hum along with the birds or sing the words if he understands bird talk. Make sure that Mr. Fagioli doesn't eat any of the curling leaves on the oleander shrubs; they're poisonous. If he's hungry, tell him to munch on a banana leaf, but not one from the wallpaper in the Polo Lounge."

"Is all that supposed to be funny?" Linguine said with a menacing look.

"Uh, no, just a little levity."

"Lose it. We don't want to leave the Lincoln at the airport, so you can take us, right, chauffeur?"

"Sure. But before we leave, when you get to LA, you'll be arriving at Gate 49A at LAX. Go to the luggage level, two floors below the concourse. Continue to baggage claim, where you retrieve your suitcases. Although you might want to take that violin case on the plane and stick it in the overhead area; it might get messed up during the baggage handling. After you get your bags, go to the blue van stop area on the center traffic island and grab an airport limo. Look for the vehicles that are red with yellow lettering—Chequer Van, it's called. You get a discount for parties of three or more. Mention my name; I know the owner. I've arranged for them to be at your disposal and take you directly to the Beverly Hills Hotel, with no stops on the way. You'll have the limo to yourselves."

"Okay, sounds great." Linguine seemed pleased.

"Also, they'll drive you to the Premature Burial Offices for your meeting with the publisher, Vincent March, on Monday."

"Hopefully it will be a successful conference."

"By the way, who plays the violin?" Mechanix asked.

"That's me, Fagioli."

The foursome, at the advice of the red limousine owner, left immediately for the airport to allow enough time for an unforeseen accident or traffic jam.

Tender was coming around, and his head was thumping. He had a golf-ball-sized lump on his noggin as if he had been the target at the end of a Jack Nicklaus 285-yard drive off the tee at the Masters in Augusta, Georgia. He raised slowly and saw that the desk drawer was ajar. He looked inside and discovered the rough draft missing. The phone pad was still open to the King Bench address, but oddly there was no phone number. Tender decided that he needed to get over there after visiting his home and office on Churchfield Lane. Tender also grabbed the picture of the quartet in front of the dark stretch and instinctively took the red-and-yellow business card.

First, he would uncover three aspirin—two never did the job—and then call Bea.

Tender told her the whole story, but she couldn't respond in kind because her mouth was full of gauze, and her body was full of pain pills. Dr. Wunderman had determined that her problem wasn't with one tooth but all four of her wisdom teeth, and he had extracted them. Consequently, Aunt Beryl said that Tender's fiancée couldn't go anywhere and expressed her and Bea's combined sentiment that he be careful. Tender balked at their attempt to get him to go to Johns Hopkins Hospital, or at least come to Armistead. He said he would be fine and had to follow a lead. Before hanging up, he wished Bea, through Aunt Beryl, a speedy recovery.

CHAPTER 9

Saturday, 4:45 p.m. EST
American Airlines Flight 117
New York to Los Angeles

Vicki Venom sat back down in her seat—seat D, row 29—after visiting the rear restroom, where she had just lost the peanuts and a double Dewar's and club soda with ice and a lemon twist that she had consumed. The Scotch drink was probably what had put her over the hump. One of the stewardesses had jammed a cart against the door, and it had taken six minutes to get it out of the way. She felt the flight attendant had done it on purpose because of Vicki's demand for a yellow citrus peel exactly an inch long.

Mrs. Venom hated to fly but had to see Vincent, so she endured. She had requested a chair in coach, which was less expensive than first-class; she had learned to be frugal, having grown up in a dairy-farming town in a remote area of Pennsylvania called Ulster. Although, her husband had always had extravagance as part of his nature, which Vicki did not mind as a part of their existence. She had also told the airline reservationist to put her near an exit. They accommodated her quite well, considering it was a last-minute request to fly to Los Angeles.

She decided to try to get some sleep, even though the person beside her, a man with a slender frame, short legs, and a skinny face and sporting a pointed nose, wanted to gab. The man reminded her of a weasel, so she ignored his advances. Mrs. Venom had come from a meager background but had garnered some of the snobbery at which her famous spouse was so adept. She positioned herself so that her back was to the talking bore. Before nodding off, she took two books out of the plastic bag purchased at a downtown Baltimore bookstore and started to leaf through one. Her eyelids were soon drooping, so she returned the reference material to the bag—there was no need to flip through the second book because it was identical to the other one.

"Linguine, did you see what the stewardess is serving?"

"When I asked her if there was any calamari, manicotti, or stuffed shells, she said that the airline chef made cream of crab soup and crab imperial, so that's what we're eating unless we want to starve. She didn't even know that calamari was squid—thought it was clams."

"I think I'm gonna turn into a crab," Fagioli said.

"How's Don Vermicelli over there?"

"My don is sleeping."

"Before we go to Premature Burial, I want to get a new suit down on Rodeo Drive."

"Can we go to Hollywood?"

"Yes, of course, but I think that at some point we should go over to one of the Pacific Ocean beaches, maybe Marina Del Rey or Malibu. It will be good for Don Vermicelli to breathe the clean, crisp sea air into his damaged lungs."

"Malibu Beach—let's go there. I want to see the surfers hang ten," Fagioli said.

"Possibly. Do you know what 'hang ten' means? I learned it during my previous time at UCLA. It's when the surfers ride the front of the long surfboard with all of their toes out over the nose. And if they aren't quite brave enough for that, a hang five will suffice.

"Hang five?"

"One foot back, only five toes over the nose."

"Oh, boy, those surf boys are good!"

"Pull that blanket up on Don Vermicelli. Please order me a Glenlivet and water on the rocks. I need to use the lavatory."

"Say *ciao* to the pilot!"

CHAPTER 10

Saturday, 4:45 p.m. EST
The Block, Downtown Baltimore

Tender's turf accountant wasn't expecting the offhand visit from one of his better customers, but he took Tender's wager on the fifth race at Laurel Park on a horse named Never Finish. Tender knew it would be a $3,500 payout on a $350 expenditure. The bet was accepted by way of an IOU; Tender was always good for it. He couldn't pass up the challenge, as he was fond of classifying the process. If he hit the winner, he and Bea could go on a cruise to Alaska for their honeymoon. Tender wouldn't mention anything if the racehorse—endorsed by the bookmaker as being a descendant from the breed bred from a cross between an Arabian stallion and English mare—finished at *show* or *worse*.

Tender's horse-betting nature was suckled as a teenager, using an unscrupulous adult to make his wagers, one who always kept a percentage of Tender's winnings. All this went down near his hometown in Florida at a racetrack that opened in 1926, originally called Tampa Downs, and renamed Sunshine Park in 1947. In the '50s, the racecourse became a popular allurement to sportswriters working spring training in the Sunshine State. Baseball writers such as Grantland Rice and Red Smith dubbed the track the "Santa Anita of the South." Most times, Tender wished he could appreciate horses for the noble animals that they were instead of how fast they could run.

Tender left the office of the gambler's best friend/worst enemy and headed farther down the Block toward a building with an Archer Arms emblem over the front door.

King Bench's name was on the mailbox to room 1983, a novel number considering there were only a total of six mail slots. There was no lobby in the building, just rickety stairs leading up to the second floor. At the top, there was a sign on the wall, "1981 to 1983," with an arrow pointing left. On the chipped plaster of the opposite wing was "1984 to 1986," suggesting the visitor hang a right.

Tender walked cautiously down the hallway covered with old green carpet that was full of holes and wearing threads sticking out in every direction. He found a doorway at the end of the hall, the one that he was seeking.

He reached out to grab the nickel-plated knocker and realized that there was light coming through the slightly cracked-open door. Tender pushed the portal until the apartment was exposed. He first noticed a bed, covers messed, flush against the wall and beneath an open window that led to a fire escape. The curtains were flying from the stiff breeze, and the room was as frigid as the enclosed quarters of many corpses at the city morgue. Strangely, the shabby, brown-and-blue Oriental throw rug, the only floor covering in the room, situated in front of the bunk, was ruffled. Tender concluded a struggle had recently taken place.

On the right side of the chamber was an entrance to the powder room. Tacked to the back of the toilet-room door was a poster of Marlboro Country, the only decorative item in the place.

On the left was a counter with just enough space between it and the red-and-white checkered wallpaper for a body to enter the kitchen beside the countertop. Tender tuned his audio senses and heard what he thought was dripping water coming from the restroom. He walked closer, entered the headquarters of the crapper, and, using his "T. T." monogrammed handkerchief, turned off the spigot that was allowing water to slowly trickle down the drain. The bathroom floor in front of the tub was semi-wet and held a twisted towel, and the shower curtain with yellow daisies was pushed back as if someone had recently taken a shower. The rest of the floor was dry as a bone, and in some sections, the wood was splintering.

Tender next found his way to the final area of the three-room apartment, the kitchen. There, he found tragedy: dead legs dressed in khakis—camouflage style, like a soldier might wear—sticking out from the opposite side of the counter. The remainder of the body revealed a head with long, unkempt golden hair, which reminded Tender of some of the surfers he used to see on the beach at Venice in California. The torso was covered with a plain white T-shirt, the left sleeve ripped. A pack of Winstons was on the floor next to the individual's left shoulder. Tender assumed that the cigs were kept in the sleeve for easy access.

There was also a dictionary tied to his right arm, as in Jake's case, but this one was the paperback version. He turned the body over with his right foot, and the word definer was Webster's Compact Dictionary. Tender also saw that there was a small bullet hole right between the eyes, like the one that Venom was outfitted in at his temporary resting place behind the huge green garbage can downtown. Tender also detected foam, as heavy as that from a rabid dog, caked around the victim's mouth, which was wide open. King Bench, assuming this was him, on more than one occasion, forgot to brush after meals. Oh, man!

PI Tender moved quickly to find a phone and call the police. It wasn't necessary. When he turned around, a pair of .38 Specials, held by two of the Baltimore Police Department's finest uniform cops, were pointed right at him.

"Down on the floor, scumbag."

Lieutenant Ripken Omaha was upstairs at the station house waiting for the desk sergeant to okay the release of his private detective friend, Tim Tender. He had convinced the arresting officers and the BPD brass that the PI wasn't responsible for King Bench's demise.

Suicide was again ruled out; no pistol was located at the Archer Arms. Omaha had just gotten back from the crime scene and was almost sure it was a .22 slug lodged in the drug pimp's cranium, most likely a bullet from the same gun used on Jake Venom. Omaha was waiting on ballistics and the report from the medical examiner. Given the foam around the mouth, he wondered whether King had been poisoned or drugged.

"Thanks for bailing me out, Rip," Tender said gratefully.

"No problem, PI. What were you doing at the Archer Arms?"

"Following a lead that I received at Vicki Venom's. I finally gained access to Jake's office and found Bench's name in Venom's phone register." Tender didn't see any reason to tell Omaha that the permission to enter the sanctuary of the terror novelist wasn't given by his widow. The missing rough draft, the limousine company's card, the photo, and the speed bump he had involuntarily collected were facts that he also kept under wraps for the time being.

"What lead would that be?"

"The word 'Cola' under King Bench's name has to mean that he was the middleman for Jake's nose-sniffing practice, huh?"

"Cola, Coke. Makes sense."

"And judging from where Bench lived, he had to be a runner, not a supplier. Get any word from the M.E. or ballistics? Has to be the same Beretta Minx as Jake's, huh?"

"That's what I think—inside straight. We knew that King was a small-timer, did some panhandling, and has a sheet for grifting and a little forgery, things like that. We never had him tabbed as drug middleman, though."

"Branching out to bigger and better things? If he had Jake Venom as a regular, the big money was possible. Any message in the Webster's?"

"Right, this one came out as, 'A double-cross gets what it deserves.'"

"There's that reference again to being worthy of the fate that befell him, huh."

"If the same gun was used, we're going to start questioning the local dealers and pawnshops, see if they can remember anyone recently buying a Beretta Minx. Call me, or I'll call you and pass on the updates. Where are you gonna be later?"

"Thanks, Rip, I'll call you. Will be at Bea's aunt's place. You got the number, right?"

"Right."

Tender was on his way to the Lord Baltimore Hotel to hopefully talk to a self-employed chauffeur.

CHAPTER 11

Saturday, 6:00 p.m. CST
American Airlines Flight 1989
Chicago to Los Angeles

Mechanix was sitting comfortably in row 13, seat F, the one next to the window. He loved the takeoffs, and the higher the plane went, the better he liked it. He pretended that he was the Conqueror of the World, dictating over all the small places and small people below him who kept getting smaller. He was on a Boeing 727-200, just like the one his three clients had flown out on earlier. However, his layover was almost an hour in Chicago instead of just over a half-hour in New York. Mechanix always preferred to fly in and out of O'Hare International because the second leg of the trip was 1,745 miles and took only 4.37 hours of actual flying time, whereas the Sicilian triad's flight from New York City was 2,475 miles long, and the long hand made 6.13 clockwise revolutions around the timepiece. He was enjoying the vegetable crab soup and crab cake sandwich they were serving. Another reason he liked Chicago's Airport was that if he felt like having a Midwestern meal, he could grab a loose meat sandwich with mustard, onions, and pickles—theirs so juicy that sometimes the juice became part of his person. There was also a chance to grab a pork tenderloin on a bun with meat thicker than a Sumo wrestler was wide.

Mechanix had some business to handle in Los Angeles but also needed some time off to loosen up. Against his usual spartan tendencies, he booked a room in the hotel across from the Mann's Chinese Theater on Hollywood Boulevard: Hotel Hollywood Roosevelt, the sight of the original Academy Awards ceremony. It had a wonderful Art Deco vestibule, beautiful courtyard, and Olympic-size pool that he could enjoy, considering California's average annual temperatures of seventy degrees as a high and fifty-one degrees as a low. He could unwind with a Scotch on the rocks in the Tropicana Bar. Mechanix always drank the Johnny Walker Brand, usually the less expensive Red, but on this occasion, he promised himself that the first shot at the hotel lounge would be Johnny Black. He never added club soda or water to his drink because he felt the additives made it sissified.

Mechanix had requested the Gable/Lombard Suite because Clark Gable was one of his favorite actors. He had seen *Gone with the Wind* several times and had used Rhett Butler's famous dialogue to Scarlett O'Hara on a few losers whom he had dated. He preferred the line from the screenplay to that of the manuscript magnificently written by Margaret Mitchell. The novel at the end of the penning read, "My dear, I don't give a damn." Mechanix felt that "Frankly" at the beginning of the phrase gave it a much better punch.

"Lady, this Scotch has soda in it. I asked for it with just the booze and ice. Take it back and get me another one," Mechanix said angrily. "Can't get decent help these days. I should have watched you pour it. You know what they say about doing something right: do it yourself."

"I'm very sorry, sir. It won't happen again," the svelte stewardess said. She wore an outfit with not one wrinkle evident to the naked eye.

"See that you do, or I'll report you to the pilot." Before exiting the airplane, Mechanix did what he had promised, visiting the cockpit and verbally filing two complaints—the second one concerning getting only two chunks of ice when three were ordered. The threat never to fly American in the future after being such a loyal customer was also put forth. Although he told the ace flyboy that he would be making at least one more trip with the airlines considering the round-trip ticket purchased, Mechanix made it clear that the human source of his objections had better not be on the return trip home.

Aunt Beryl's Place
Saturday, 8:00 p.m. EST

Tender was speaking to his girl through her aunt, her new interpreter, who had a full day of trying to decipher Bea's moans and grunts, when the phone rang.

"Hello, is Private Investigator Tender there?" Lt. Omaha asked.

"Yes, just a minute," Beryl said. "Timster, it's for you."

Tender had gone to the Lord Baltimore to hopefully hook up with the owner of Mechanix's Limo Service, but he had found a note on the door stating that the agency was going to be closed for a few days due to a trip to Los Angeles, and to put a business card into the mail slot if further contact was needed. Tender had left one of his cards with a message on the back about wanting to talk to the proprietor.

"Hey, Rip, what's up? Beretta Minx as we suspected, huh?"

"Yeah, and according to the associate medical examiner who did the autopsy, the bullet didn't kill the drug distributor, but—"

"Don't tell me. Viper venom again?"

"Right, PI, but this deadly milk came from a king cobra, one originating from Thailand—southern Asia, not southern Africa. The killer must know his serpents. Gonna check out some zoos and pet stores for possible leads."

"This killer seems to be into the symbolism. Another writer, maybe? How'd the poison get inside his body?"

"Small needle hole in a vein of the right arm, just like Jake. Don't think King was a user—no tracks or chafing anywhere—and we feel that he knew his assailant.

"How's that?"

"Well, we found two paper cups with Scotch whisky on the counter next to the fridge, along with the booze bottle, in an orderly little row, one almost empty and the other almost full. Surprised you missed that."

"Your guys were on me too quick. By the way, why were they there in the first place, huh?"

"Got an anonymous phone call saying a shot was heard at the Archer Arms. The uniforms tried to talk to the neighbors but found only one home, in apartment 1984: an elderly lady with hearing aids in both ears who said she never heard a thing. She was in a world of her own. Said she used to live with an older sibling, Kurt, but he moved to London to some condos called Victory Mansions. I guess her heat wasn't working properly. Officer Newspeak relayed that she kept repeating, 'I'm *pluscold, doublepluscold.*' Strange."

"Apartment 1984, huh? Does she have anybody watching over her now?"

"No. It's sad, although she did mention that with her big brother's departure, she might be better off."

"Maybe they didn't get along."

"Anyway, we think whoever poisoned King was having a drink with him. Found a small trace of the snake poison in the sink of the restroom."

"Maybe the killer was trying to wash off a syringe and didn't turn off the handle completely. Maybe he didn't like the rotgut either? Any prints?"

"Wiped clean. Gotta go. See ya, PI."

"Okay, Rip, thanks again."

During the conversation with Omaha, Tender had decided that it was time to visit the home of movie stars, *The Beverly Hillbillies,*

and the Dodgers. His client, Vicki Venom, was making the trip to
see not Mr. March of Premature Burial Publishing but a seemingly
more personal visit with Vincent. Plus, now a suspicious limousine
driver had made the trip to the West Coast.

CHAPTER 12

Monday, 8:30 a.m. PST

The three Sicilians found a restaurant on Santa Monica Boulevard called The Palermo Near the Pacific, where they could finally get calamari, manicotti, and stuffed shells. They weren't going to wait until dinner to enjoy the specialties—breakfast was the perfect time for classic Italian. They were also successful at finding some prune juice for Don Vermicelli, even though he wanted coffee and brandy.

The Palermo served these types of delicacies morning, noon, and night. This cuisine was as good as what they usually found in Sicily. The owners, who hailed from Rome but had moved to Sicily's chief port and capital city to open a cafe called The Palermo Near the Tyrrhenian, didn't even know what cream of crab soup or crab imperial was. As they told the Sicilians, their first eating establishment had earned them enough lira to afford a move to California, a place they had always dreamt about, and they built their second food concern there.

Linguine, Fagioli, and Vermicelli were very happy that they did. The don could even get a muffuletta sandwich like the ones he used to get at Salvatore Lupa's Central Grocery in New Orleans back in 1910, a place he had lived when he had been a juvenile soldier moving up the crime tree. Lupa's muffulettas were always made traditionally, with layers of hard salami, ham, provolone, and olive salad served on a split-in-half, round roll of Italian bread. Other restaurants that he had found in Baltimore claimed to have the delicacy from the home of Mardi Gras, but they served the ingredients minus the olive salad and on rectangular bread. Jonah Vermicelli had always tried to tell them, through Linguine, that all they were serving was a submarine. They never listened, and Vermicelli eventually gave up.

"Hurry, we've got to get going. The meeting will start soon, and I want to stop on Rodeo Drive first," Linguine stated.

"Can we go to the LA Zoo later? I want to see my friends," Fagioli said.

"You mean Gita the elephant and Methuselah the alligator?"

"Plus, Herman the rhino," Fagioli said.

"Maybe after taking care of business, if Don Vermicelli isn't too tired. I would like to visit the zoo's reptile house—that's always interesting. Also, for the brass's sake at Premature Burial, the sit-down had better go the way we want it to, right?"

"That's right!"

Monday, 8:30 a.m. PST
Home of Vincent March
Santa Monica

Vicki Venom was enjoying her soft-boiled egg sitting in a twelve-karat gold-plated egg holder, a pink grapefruit mimosa, and an English muffin with blueberry preserves. She was at the two-story, salmon-colored, royal blue awninged, red-tiled roof, palatial estate of the owner and publisher at the Premature Burial Publishing Empire. She was lounging in a beige silk robe with a monogrammed *VM* over her left breast.

Vicki was looking through a pane of glass in the French doors that was cracked. She thought, *In this house of perfection.* The breakfast nook overlooked a patio with a courtyard containing a fully operating fountain at its center. There were many flower beds—red, blue, violet—and professionally manicured bushes surrounding that section of the mansion. She stared out at Santa Monica Bay.

Vincent March walked into the room wearing a three-piece, gray pinstriped, nine-hundred-dollar Calvin Klein suit. He had had his clothes imported from New York City.

"How 'bout some breakfast, Vincent?" said Vicki.

"No time. I've got a meeting this morning with the trifecta of Sicilians at the office at 10:15. I'll just have Thelma bring in some coffee. I told them 10:00, so they can talk to Price first."

"Thelma is a very good servant. Does she do windows?" Mrs. Venom said with a chuckle. "What else is the meeting about, besides what we've already discussed?"

"They think that Mario Puzo ripped off their story when he wrote *The Godfather,* and they want their manuscript published to tell the real story—about some guy named Don Jonah Vermicelli. I'll humor them with that until we get to the real subject of the conference."

"Jonah is his first name?"

"Yes, you believe it. But you know my philosophy: Never say never to anybody; no one knows where the next Robert Louis Stevenson will come from."

"Jake always said that he wished he could have written something as good as *The Strange Case of Dr. Jekyll and Mr. Hyde.*"

"A true classic. Got to run. When I get back, I'll fill you in on the Fredric Price developments."

"Yes, your conniving senior editor."

Monday, 8:30 a.m. PST
Venice Beach

Tender was just finishing his self-prepared griddle cakes, sausage links, Monterey Jack cheese slices, and caffeine at the back apartment of the little house on the Venice Canal. He had lived there during his one year of private investigating in Los Angeles. He had moved here after leaving his dorm stint at Fresno. In the past, he had picked up some tricks of the cooking trade from a head chef at the Lakeside Elementary School in Saint Petersburg. While living on his own, he developed many easy and delicious recipes. The same landlord owned the small wooden home and was now renting the rear room on a daily, weekly, or monthly basis. After Tender's 365-day stay, the homeowner could not seem to keep anyone there long enough to lease it yearly. Lucky for Tender, the apartment was available. Tender gave his friend an advance payment for two days, not knowing when he would be returning to Baltimore. He hadn't arrived until late afternoon on Sunday, satisfying a gambling urge at a layover in the Las Vegas airport.

His main objective of this day was to visit the offices of Premature Burial Publishing on Wilshire Boulevard. But first, he wanted to go down to the beach and see whether any of the same street performers and artists were still there from his 1967 year of residency in funky town. He also wanted to see if the Shelby Manufacturing Plant opened by Caroll Shelby in 1964 in Venice was still operating. He could check out some of the fastest, street-legal Mustangs ever produced, and possibly he could even find a steal.

Tender would take the small boat that the landlord supplied his guests to his rental car, a compact Ford Maverick, the only one he could afford after his stopover in the gambling capital of the West. He had lost a substantial amount of his winnings, which came from the horse who thankfully didn't live up to his name, Never Finish, at the Laurel Race Course.

Monday, 8:30 a.m. PST
Hollywood Roosevelt

Mechanix was in Los Angeles to keep tabs on his best customers through his friend at the Chequer Van Company—and to tend to some matters of necessity. He got stuck in the Shirley Temple Suite, not the Gable/Lombard, as he had requested.

He ordered a root beer after consuming his morning meal of green-pea eggs and ham. The soft drink was one he had used in a former world in the mid-sixties to dilute his LSD. This had been while staying at 710 Ashbury Street, a huge Victorian mansion in the heart of the Haight-Ashbury district in central San Francisco. He even claimed to have once gotten high with Jerry Garcia of the Grateful Dead. In 1968, the home in the Haight became a bus tour stop, which was when Mechanix decided to move to Baltimore. He had taken acid only twice in the East and said he preferred to do it in the West, his altered-state-of-awareness roots; therefore, he was going to take full advantage of his LA trip. Mechanix dropped the drug tab into the sweet liquid and laid back his head to hallucinate and hopefully reminisce.

"Hey, Gene, take my picture, will ya? You've taken everybody else's in Haight-Ashbury. I'm certainly better for your lens than Ginsberg was."

"Mechanix, can't you see that I don't have my camera? I'll have to go up to my apartment on Divisadero and get it," said the man dressed in a long-sleeve shirt with a white turtleneck underneath, sporting a short-brimmed cowboy hat and full beard.

"Okay. That'll give me enough time to get my best Day-Glo tee for the shot."

A converted 1939 International Harvester bus with swirling rainbow colors pulled up to the curb on Haight Street right beside Mechanix. The green-and-red front bumper had the words "Magic Bus" painted in the middle in white letters. Ken Kesey, the brazen novelist, got off the vehicle.

"*Mechanix, come on, get on the bus.*"

"*Where are you going? I have to wait here for Anthony to come back and take my picture.*"

"*Destination's 'Furthur.' Man, let's go. Besides, Anthony's already got a shoot goin' down with Neil Cassidy; he's better-looking than Ginsberg any day. That's why I'm driving the bus today.*

"*I know you want to be a writer, Mechanix, so I want to read you some passages from 'One Flew Over the Cuckoo's Nest.' Now, that's writing, I think somebody will want to make a movie about it one day—maybe George Cukor or Milos Forman.*"

"*Man, you're dreaming. That'll never happen. Can I drive?*" Mechanix hopped on the bus, and the state-of-the-art sound system was blaring "Purple Haze" by Hendrix. "*I can see Jimi in my mind's eye when he and the Experience were playing Monterey at the pop festival, and he fell to his knees and torched his guitar.*"

"*Yeah, Jimi's some showman. Let's go to the Whiskey A-Go-Go in LA. I think there are still some tickets left to the Doors concert tonight.*"

"*No, let's go to the Fillmore instead. Janis and Grace are supposed to sing together tonight,*" Mechanix said with anticipation.

The duo of art enthusiasts stopped by The Print Mint, and Mechanix picked up a Wes Wilson original artwork of the Dead, complete with the skeleton. He had a hard time getting Kesey out of the store with wall-to-wall unique lettered and rainbow-colored posters; Kesey had met Wavy Gravy, an ex-member of Ken's Merry Prankster group, and they were trying to dream up some sort of monkeyshine to play on somebody. Mechanix decided to walk down to the Fillmore.

As he was hoofing by the Avalon, he could hear Country Joe and the Fish playing their anti–Vietnam War song, "I Feel like I'm Fixin' to Die Rag," so he popped in.

When he finally arrived at the Fillmore, Mechanix saw that the two rock queens had canceled, and some guy named Carlos Santana and his band were a last-second fill-in. Mechanix went straight to Graham's office to protest.

Bill was dressed in a dark pullover sweater that matched his dark, full head of hair, and a sleeve was pushed up to just below each elbow. He had a wide grin on his face that immediately changed to a strong scowl when Mechanix walked into his poster-laden suite—the counterculture art was on the walls, the ceiling, everywhere. Mr. Graham had always said to everyone that artists like Wes Wilson, Bonnie MacLean, Stanley Mouse, Rick Griffin, and many others had furnished their visions and provided some of the most original and vital American art of the twentieth century.

"What do you want, Mechanix?"

"Man, where's Janis? Where's Grace?"

"Grace got sick, has laryngitis, and Janis is too stoned. I replaced them with this new group, Santana Blues Band; they play Latin rock. Man, I heard them auditioning earlier, and they're gonna be big one day."

"No way that'll ever happen. I want to hear some acid rock, man."

"Then go over to The Whiskey and see Morrison, Manzarek, Krieger, and Densmore. Maybe you and Jim can have a shot of Jack Black together. Tonight, The Fillmore is gonna jam on salsa rock."

Mechanix thought that he was getting hungry, so he decided to cross Haight Street to the Panhandle and see if the Diggers would give him some grub. As he stumbled into the street, he looked up, and the International Harvester was coming right for him. It wasn't being driven by Kesey or Cassidy but an Asian. It had a red flag that contained a yellow star in its middle flying from each of the front fenders.

The vehicle's wheelman had a crazy look on his face; finally, Mechanix recognized the face that he had seen on many posters in Vietnam during his six-month stint in the jungles of southeast Asia: it was Ho Chi Minh, scraggly beard jutting down from his chin and a red poppy flower stuck behind each ear. Morris Mechanix didn't have time to get out of the way.

As he was dying in his illusion, the first time it had ever happened, he could hear Ho screaming in English, "You gotta be with us, man, or *you're out, you're dead." Then the Vietnamese Communist leader doused Morris with napalm jelly and threw a match.*

   Mechanix wanted the terrible trip to stop, but unfortunately, he'd have to ride it out.

   Mechanix finally came around and felt his face—there was no blood, burned skin, or dented parts. He quickly checked up and down his body; he was fine. For a while, during his lapse into self-inflicted dementia, he thought he might end up on a metal slab back at Dr. Smith's Free Clinic in Haight-Ashbury. He swore to himself. No more dropping acid.

CHAPTER 13

Monday, 10:00 a.m. PST
Premature Burial Offices
Wilshire Boulevard

Fredric Price had just buzzed his secretary to send in the three Sicilians. He didn't want to talk to them, but Vincent March hadn't arrived yet. The trio was getting impatient, and considering the subject matter of their manuscript, the editor thought that even though he felt they were no threat, maybe to be safe, he shouldn't keep them waiting any longer than necessary. Price was British and a smallish man, only rising to the height of five-foot-two and weighing in at about eleven stones, but he had lofty goals and aspirations that he hoped would be realized at the expense of his boss.

"Good morning, Mr. Price. My name is Aldo Linguine, and these are my associates, Mr. Fagioli and Don Vermicelli. The don is why we are here; this is his life story. Is Mr. March here yet?" Linguine handed the editor a copy of the manuscript with the title *The Sicilian Godfather* and the byline *Jonah Vermicelli*. The paper also contained a header with just the letter *M* centered.

Fredric Price took the story and read a few pages, right away figuring the *M* had to stand for *Mob* or *Mafioso,* some term depicting the crime syndicate. *Moron,* as far as he was concerned, would be more appropriate—three broken-down hoods claiming that Mario

Puzo had stolen their idea. Ridiculous. But he would be professional and stall them until the owner and publisher arrived.

The meeting ended abruptly with three statements from the senior editor. "Gentlemen, our secretary, Hesta Perrine, has informed me that Mr. March has arrived and wants to talk to you right away. Thank you for coming by; I'm sure we'll meet again in the future. Let me tell him that you're here."

"Vincent, the Sicilians are here to see you; I'm going to Malibu, Topanga Beach, to take some contracts over to E. MacBane about the script *Queenie's Ransom.*"

Two men from Sicily barged their way into the office, each one giving a slight bump to Price. Vermicelli waited in a comfy chair outside in the anteroom.

"Excuse me," Linguine said.

"Me too," Fagioli added.

"You're going where, Fredric?" March asked.

"To MacBane's motel in Topanga. Remember? We discussed it previously."

"Right."

"I'll see you later," Price said.

"Right, Fredric." As the senior editor left his office, Vincent picked up the phone and made a quick call before talking to his guests. When he hung up, he said, "Mr. Linguine and Mr. Fagioli, how are you today?"

"Fine, Mr. March. If we can come to an agreement, the day will become much brighter."

"Oh, I'm sure we will, sir. Is Mr. Vermicelli with you?"

"Yes, he's resting in your lobby. Pasta brought his instrument in the violin case to play your tune."

"No, we won't need anything that sophisticated; we already have a smaller device for him to perform with. Now, to the business at hand. Mr. Price has told me that your story is not one that he would be interested in at this time."

"What about this bum Putzo stealing my don's story?" Pasta E. Fagioli said, agitated.

"What about that, Mr. March?" Linguine said with even more anxiety.

"Piracy in these cases is covered by your copyright."

"Copyright? We don't know of such things."

"The minute you put a piece of writing to paper, it is considered copyrighted, and it is your decision what to do with it. There's an unwritten code among people in the literary business that the author's work is his or hers alone to distribute in any manner that he or she wishes. Thievery is something that just doesn't happen that frequently, but it has been known to take place."

"Yes, to Mr. Vermicelli," Linguine stated.

"I don't think so," March responded.

"You know the line from *The Godfather* spoken by Don Corleone: 'A lawyer with a briefcase can steal more than a hundred men with guns.' Don Vermicelli originated that line of dialogue in this manner: *'Un consigliere con una valigia puo rubare piu di mille soldati con stufe.'* I'll translate it into English: 'A counselor with a valise can thieve more than a thousand soldiers with heaters.'"

"Well, gentlemen, for extra protection, even fifty years after the author's life ends, you should have sent the proper payment and form with a copy of your work to the Register of Copyrights at the Library of Congress in Washington, DC; of course, according to you three, it's a little late."

Miss Perrine rang March and told him that there was a PI waiting for him.

"A private investigator? What does he want?"

"Sir, he says he is working for Mrs. Venom, huh."

"What do you mean, huh?"

"That's what he keeps saying at the end of his statements. Sorry, huh."

"Miss Perrine, please. It must be Tim Tender. Show him in." March wondered what Tender was doing at his agency. "I'm sorry, gentlemen, but as you can see, it's becoming a busy morning. Good luck, and don't forget that rejection is a part of writing, but if you can complete the business that we earlier discussed, maybe I can help achieve your publishing goals."

The trio of Sicilians left Premature Burial Publishing after telling the owner that they knew how to deal with such matters. Before leaving, they asked for directions to the J. Paul Getty Museum on Pacific Coast Highway in Malibu. They decided to give the Chequer Van limo driver the rest of the day off. Publisher March gave them a very specific route to take to find what they were looking for and passed them some rental car keys.

"Mr. March, how are you today, huh?"

"Mr. Tender, nice to see you again."

"First, I'd like to thank you for your recommendation on my behalf to the widow Venom, huh."

"My pleasure. Any progress in the dearly departed Jake Venom's case?"

"Everything's Jake in Jake's murder case."

"Is that your vain attempt at humor?"

"Sorry, a little shamus silliness, huh?"

"You say 'huh' a lot, did you know that?"

"Just something I voice without really thinking about it, huh."

"You should work on that," March said.

"Thank you, I will. The Baltimore PD has confirmed a .22 Beretta Minx as the deadly weapon."

"Any suspects?"

"No, not yet, but another killing took place on Saturday in downtown Baltimore," Tender said.

"Another author?"

"A small-time hood. Cops think he was a drug runner. Like Mr. Venom, he had a .22 short stuck in his head." Tender decided not to mention the snake poisons yet.

"Coincidence?"

"I don't think so, Mr. March. The victim's name was King Bench, and the funny thing was that his name and address were in Jake Venom's phone pad. Is Mrs. Venom here? She told me she was coming out here to see you—Vincent! To be consoled, I presume."

"Yes, she's very upset about Jake's death. You can understand."

"Absolutely. So, is she here?"

"Uh—uh, no. She's staying at my place in Santa Monica."

"Your place?"

"Yes, I have plenty of room—five bedrooms, four bathrooms. She can have her own. I didn't see any reason for her to stay in an unfriendly hotel by herself."

"Right. Can I drive out and talk to her, update her on the case, see if she knew anything about King Bench?"

"Are you suggesting Jake was on drugs?"

"I'm not suggesting anything right now. You never received his latest story. What was it called?"

"*The Godfather of Bane*. Vick and I assumed the killer stole it. Have the police found it?"

Tender immediately noticed how the publisher referred to Mrs. Venom. He felt that all the first naming was a little too casual for a supposed relationship spawned from a business arrangement with the now-deceased master storyteller of horror. And March's reference to "Vick" concerning Mrs. Venom seemed even more like a pet name. "No, the elusive manuscript hasn't been located."

"Vick and I are flying back to Baltimore Wednesday to attend Jake's funerals, so I don't think it's a good idea that you bother her now. Why don't you have some compassion and at least wait until after the ceremonies to badger her?"

"You can speak for her in this situation, huh?"

"If you feel it necessary, I'll give you my phone number, and you can ask her yourself."

"Thank you, I will. By the way, who were those three men who just left here? For some reason, they look familiar."

"Nobody important."

After Tender left, Vincent March told his administrative assistant not to forward any calls unless "extreme emergency" was part of the dialogue from the person talking on the other end.

Vincent March was correct in his assessment of Vicki Venom's refusal to see Tender; she accused him of spying on her. After Tender filled her in about the bump he received on his head in Jake's office, and the fact that the rough draft copy of *Tender Nightmare* was also now missing from the author's desk, the widow threatened him with a breaking-and-entering charge and removal from the case. He bowed to his instincts and left her alone. For the time being.

Tender had a dilemma: either go back to Venice Beach and watch some roller-skating, bikini-style, or find some off-track wagering. Possibly both.

Before departing the publishing house, he had inquired about why there were so few people on duty in the department. The agency, apart from the inner suites of the senior editor and the owner-publisher, seemed to be one large room, with Miss Perrine's desk located at the forefront of working spaces for a staff of about twelve bodies. Counting the secretary, there were only four underlings in attendance. Layoffs, as offered by the administrative assistant while standing by the water cooler with no one to talk to, was the reason divulged.

Premature Burial Publishing possibly having financial problems? Curious, Tender thought.

Monday 1:00 p.m. PST
Malibu

Mechanix had sobered up. He had just received a call from his friend at the Chequer Van Company about the triad of Sicilians relieving him of his transportation service and their wish to go to Malibu. Funny thing: Mechanix had already planned to go to Calabasas, near Malibu, to a large auto parts store on the corner of Calabasas Road and Mulholland Drive that carried items for vehicles of the 1959 vintage, like his GMC truck. It was the only organization in the country where he was able to locate such parts. He was a little embarrassed about having to drive there in the Plymouth Duster, with the awful white sidewall tires, that he had rented at the last possible minute.

Someone had stolen from him—a concept with which he seemed to be getting familiar and extremely irritated. This time, it was the original cigar lighter from his rig. He couldn't fathom the fact that he may have simply lost it. How could he? His lips never touched a cigar or cigarette, or any tobacco for that matter, so he would have had no reason to even touch the small flamer. The only association he had ever had with fire was as "Mr. Zippo" in Vietnam—he was a flamethrower, a job description that he had always tried to forget. In fact, like most everyone else not even acknowledging veterans of the war that should never have been, he was trying to disregard the entire horrid experience. Unfortunately, it wouldn't go away. He had gained too many bad hang-ups from the war.

After fifteen minutes of solid negotiating, Mechanix bought the lighter for what he perceived to be a semi-reasonable price and drove off to see if he could locate his best customers.

CHAPTER 14

Tuesday, 8:00 a.m. PST
Venice Beach

Tender was enjoying his magic marshmallow crescent puffs that he had made, starting with Pillsbury's refrigerated crescent dinner rolls. He was using Edna Holmgren's 1969 Pillsbury Bake-Off grand-prize-winning recipe, with ingredients cut to one-quarter, yielding only four rolls instead of the sixteen Edna's formula made. The only item that he left out was the cinnamon she used—a spice that gave him an allergic reaction and would create a red welt the size of a maraschino cherry.

Bea E. Hopkins had entered the competition once in 1966 after they had moved the contest from October to February, not having a bake-off in 1965. Her entry was in the "simple side dishes" category with her famous green bean casserole, one of Tender's favorites because of the cheese used in the mix; he's a cheese freak. His fiancée's vegetable blueprint was a marvelous mixture: Green Giant green beans (a qualifying brand), diced onions sautéed in butter (not margarine) until clear, one can of cream of mushroom soup (Campbell's if possible), two or three slices of bread (any shade), and six or seven slices of American cheese melted on the top. Marvelous eating.

Unfortunately, Bea lost out in 1966 to a recipe called "Golden Gate Snack Bread"—Tender's girlfriend had told him that she felt like throwing that particular recipe off the bridge that carried the same name, and stuffing that snack bread where the sun didn't shine. However, she did admit that she may have screwed up by using frozen beans instead of the canned variety.

Tender had just taken a sip of java and then a bite of Cracker Barrel's Vermont sharp, the brand he preferred, when he opened the *Los Angeles Times* to the local section and almost gagged on his cheese. His well-trained eyes immediately focused on a headline.

Senior editor of Premature Burial Publishing found dead on the rocks near Santa Monica

Tender went on to read about how Fredric Price was discovered dead by a bullet from an unknown weapon. The article further revealed that an unusual occurrence had been discovered at the crime scene by Lieutenant Koufax Sands, the detective in charge of the matter. Tender recognized the city cop's name. The feature did not mention what that odd circumstance was, but Tender had a pretty good idea: highlighted words in a dictionary. He quickly gulped his coffee and stuffed the remainder of the cheddar and moon-shaped rolls of lightness into his mouth together, two food delicacies that he usually enjoyed savoring each morsel. He dressed in one of his Philip Marlowe best.

After starting the ignition of the Maverick, he pointed the wheel to the north and hit the Pacific Coast Highway, hoping to locate Lt. Sands of the Santa Monica Police Department, an old acquaintance. Tender had once solved a case before Sands was able to come up with the solution, and it had cost the California cop, according to him, a promotion to captain. No love was lost between the two justice seekers from different coasts.

Tuesday, 10:00 a.m. PST
Santa Monica Police Department

"*Gumshoe* Tender, why are you on the West Coast? I thought you were safely tucked away in Baltimore, where you'd stay out of my hair."

"*Flatfoot* Sands, what hair are you referring to? You're as bald as a cue ball, as Rip would say, huh."

"How's Ripken Omaha doin' these days? He's a good cop. Has he called in sick yet?"

"Great cop, and he's fine. Nope, still works even when he's ill."

"What can I do for you?" Lt. Sands asked.

"Read about a body found near here yesterday."

"Yes, between Topanga Beach and the I-10 Freeway off State Road 1; found the corpse stuck among some large rocks, quite a bit of skin lost from the fall I imagine. Why, what's it to you?"

"Or the push, you mean. You find a .22 short between his eyes, huh?"

"How'd you know that?"

"Came from a Beretta Minx?"

"That's right."

"Webster's Dictionary tied to his right arm?"

"How do you know those things? And it was a Doubleday Dictionary."

"You mean the guy who supposedly invented the great American pastime also published reference books, huh?"

"No, now you're as dumb as a cue ball. Frank Doubleday's company, not Abner's," Sands said.

"Touché. I was just kidding."

"Keep the wise-guy stuff for your buddy, Omaha, will ya."

"Did the dictionary have any words highlighted in it? One of the words is a form of *deserve*, right?" Tender thought for sure that word would be emphasized.

"Along that line. It's starting to sound like you've experienced a similar case. The message said, 'A blackmailer gets what is coming to him.'"

"Did your M.E. find snake venom in the system?" said Tender.

"No. Why do you say that?"

"You sure?"

"Yes, yes." Sands was getting irritated.

"You know the terror writer, Jake Venom?" Tender said.

"I've read his book *The Fascist Dean*."

"Me too. I think we bought 50 percent of the paperbacks that were sold. Not one of his better efforts. Did you see Cronkite's report and then short biography on Jake Venom on CBS?"

"Don't watch the television news; I don't want to see and hear the same stuff I live every day. What about Venom?"

"Jake and a small-time hood, which just happened to have his name and address in Venom's telly register, were both shot in the same manner as the senior editor of Premature Burial Publishing, which ironically is the company that distributes Venom's books. But the horror writer and the punk were done in by snake juice, not the .22 short. Sudanese red cobra for Venom and king cobra for King Bench were the vipers of record."

"The MO seems to be the same except for the snakes. Odd," said Lt. Sands.

"In my experience, serial killers—if that's what this scum is— don't usually change their method," Tender returned.

"Maybe your professed coast-to-coast killer couldn't manage to get a snake out here and decided just to plug Price."

"Baltimore PD thinks the snakes were used to try to make some sort of point."

"What point would that be?" asked Sands.

"Haven't quite figured that out yet. I think it's obvious it has to do with the names Venom and King. Maybe some type of literary symbolism."

"Nothing's ever taken for granted. I have to go to the LAPD on Culver Boulevard. The captain's having a briefing about Price's killing at eleven. I should be handling that briefing. Got a car here?"

"Yes, a Ford Maverick parked outside," Tender said, somewhat embarrassed.

"A Maverick! You keep it in front or back of the nursing home?"

"It's the only thing the rental company had left, huh? I have a flight back to Baltimore soon. Jake Venom's two funerals are taking place on Thursday."

"Two funerals?"

"Don't ask! Thanks for the information, Sands."

"Drive safe, Tender."

Lieutenant Sands of Santa Monica had told Tender that both Vincent March and Vicki Venom had airtight alibis at the time of Fredric Price's demise: March's secretary, Hesta Perrine, had said that he was at Premature Burial; March's housekeeper, Thelma, who had been his employee for many years, verified Mrs. Venom's whereabouts as being at the publisher's home all day Monday. Sands also said that no prints had been evident at the scene, and the Beretta Minx hadn't turned up.

CHAPTER 15

Thursday, 11:00 a.m. EST
West Russell Street
Baltimore

Tender was on his way to Westminster Presbyterian Church and Cemetery, and then on to the Edgar Allan Poe House to scope out the duo of funerals and scatterings of the late, great terror author Jake Venom. Tender had not been invited to attend but wanted to see who showed up and how they reacted. He was wearing his all-black Philip Marlowe, not wanting to look out of place in case he was spotted. The first leg of the last rites and ash dispensing was set for 1:00 p.m. at Westminster, the locale of Edgar Allan Poe's earthly entombment. The itinerary had been listed in Wednesday's *Baltimore Sun*. Then the ceremonies would shift to the one-time home of the writer of such wonderful poems as "The Conqueror Worm" and "The Sleeper." Poe had lived in the two-bay, two-and-a-half-story brick building with his aunt, Maria Clemm, and her daughter, Virginia, Edgar's cousin, whom he later wed. She was only fourteen at the time—quite young for a union with a twenty-seven-year-old, Tender felt.

Tender was hungry, so he stopped at a burger place to get some nourishment.

"Move for'd, hon!" the counter person said.

Tender didn't budge.

"S'mour, you tarred? Move ford and order, unnersteand!

"Ah, she's talking Bawlamerese—must be from south Baltimore," Tender whispered to himself. He deduced that the girl behind the shiny-clean counter must've wanted him to order, especially considering that there was no one else remaining in the line except him. "I'll have a cheeseburger, double cheese; fries, hot, please; and a Coke, lots of ice."

"Don't want no arn juice? Good fer ya, hon. Put awl in yer crankcase."

Tender stood and stared, trying to decipher what the employee had just said.

"Whyon't ya get a cammer and take some pictures?"

"Oh—no, none of that." Tender decided no was the best response. He did hear the word juice and knew he didn't want any other liquid than Coke. "Where's your restroom, huh?"

"Baffroom's don the hall, hon! Cleanest tawlits in Balamer."

He took care of his business at hand in the *baffroom*, and then he sat down and finished his fast food.

Bea was efficient with how some Baltimore natives communicated, and she had tried to teach Tender some words. He remembered just three. Tender spoke to the counter operative: "Hey, hon! the fries were *turble*, cold, worst I ever tasted in the whole state of *Merlin*."

She responded, "Jump in yer mahsheen and hit the payment. Next time, go to a semlem."

Tender motored his Mustang toward the celebrity-attended twin dispersals of Jake's sooty remains.

Thursday, 1:00 p.m. EST
Westminster Church and Cemetery
West Fayette Street

Tender moved toward the cemetery and noticed a long black limousine, a Continental, with a flag of Italy extended from each front fender. The banners were swaying in the stiff breeze that had developed on that cold, overcast morning.

Suddenly, he remembered and took out the photo from the inside pocket of his jacket that he had found at Venom's home. It was the same stretch—it had to be. The vehicle stood out from the rest of the luxury vehicles because of the green, white, and red emblems. He figured the four men in the picture had to be at the funeral. The long auto was sitting directly in front of the Egyptian-style iron gate that Tender had to open to enter the cemetery. He pondered briefly about whether Amenhotep, an architect in Egyptian mythology elevated to the god of building, may have supplied the design for this means of access. He said in a low tone, "Why do I think of such things?"

Tender moved undetected to the rear of a tall headstone, where he was able to hear and observe the proceedings. He knew that Jake Venom had many celebrities as friends, and several of them were in attendance:

Lee Marvin did make the first funeral and was standing next to his costar in *The Dirty Dozen*, Ernest Borgnine; stars of *The Taming of the Shrew*, Liz Taylor and Dick Burton seemed to be arguing about something; Crosby and Hope were bookending Dorothy Lamour; the three ballplaying Robinsons, Frank, Brooks and Jackie, in from Brooklyn, were there; and Vincent Price was standing nervously, pale-looking but strong-chinned, his hair wispy. Price was holding a life-sized placard of his departed colleague Boris Karloff. There was a sort of heavy mist around just Vinnie; possibly it followed him from a lagoon he may have wandered by.

And in the audience were three men whom Tender was standing nearest to, enabling him to hear some of their conversation about a possible movie deal in the future: Francis Coppola, Marlon Brando, and Mario Puzo.

Tender then noticed a trio of what he perceived to be Italian men who matched perfectly the chaps in his photograph. The oldest of the three seemed to be staring darts at Mister Puzo.

The Baltimore district attorney and commissioner of police were also present.

The service began with Mrs. Venom holding a golden urn. She was positioned behind a podium at the opposite end of Edgar's headstone. Vincent March was standing beside her, offering a hand to Vick's shoulder. Tender listened.

"Dear Jake so loved the writings of Edgar Allan Poe, and the reading and relishing of some of Poe's greatest—'The Tell-Tale Heart,' 'Ligeia,' 'The Fall of the House of Usher,' 'The Raven,' et cetera—are the tales and poems that got him started on the path to his horror greatness," Vicki Venom said at the start of her eulogy. "*Tender Nightmare*, his crowning achievement, will be forever known as his legacy."

Mrs. Venom continued her homage to her late husband. "The beginning of 'Ligeia' states words supposedly written by Joseph Glanvill, famous for his religious works and discourses on spiritual signs and eternal souls, which Jake said that Poe may have indeed made up himself but attributed to the writer of the seventeenth century: 'And the will therein lieth, which dieth not. Who knoweth the mysteries of the will, with its vigor—' My will, will forever be linked with Jake's, and he will take care of me with his will, spiritually?"

Again, she quoted Edgar: "'During the whole of a dull, dark, and soundless day in the autumn of the year'—"

Suddenly, the star of many a script transferred from stories by Poe, Vincent Price, screamed out, "That's my line!"

"No, Vinnie, you played Sir Roderick Usher, brother to Lady Madeline, in Corman's *House of Usher*, remember? That was not your line at all; it belonged to the narrator, Roderick's boyhood companion, in Mr. Poe's tale."

"Oh, right. Sorry. I've been so preoccupied lately that I think I'm almost losing my mind. I apologize for the interruption," Price said.

Tender thought for a moment how Roger Corman, the director of the excitingly scary flick, one that had given Tender a nightmare after his viewing in his later teen years, had taken privileges apart from the brilliant short story, "The Fall of the House of Usher," such as making the narrator the fiancé of Madeline and having the house burn as it was immersed by the murky lake. In Poe's telling, the "blood-red moon shining through the worm-like bisection in the Usher estate" provided the contrast between fire and water.

Vicki continued. "I, devoted wife of Jake Venom, dedicate half of these ashes to this hallowed ground." She spread them over Poe's grave, careful to keep the remaining half in the urn. "Okay, everyone, now we need to head over to Amity Street to 'the little house in the lowly street with the lovely name,' as Edgar Allan Poe referred to it. We will continue the observances. First ones there get the best view of the final spreading."

CHAPTER 16

Thursday, 1:45 p.m. EST
Lord Baltimore Hotel
20 West Baltimore Street

Tender sat in his car across the street from the Lord Baltimore Hotel and watched the three Sicilians walk into the building. He was beginning to believe that there were a lot of coincidences developing in the Venom, Bench, and Price cases. The trio of foreigners had a room in the same classically ornamented architecture of the highrise structure that held the Mechanix Limousine Agency. Curious.

Tender had followed them from the first half of Jake Venom's dual cremation ceremonies. They didn't make the short, five-minute trip to the Poe house. When Tender began to trail them on West Fayette, instead of heading in the direction of North Amity Street, the boss of all bosses and his loyal soldiers in their black limousine hung a right on North Charles toward West Baltimore Street. Whoever was driving must have wanted to make sure to not miss any street signs, motoring along at only fifteen miles per hour.

Tender decided that even though darkness had yet to surround the downtown and port areas, he would perform a part of his job that he usually found unexciting but sometimes essential: a stakeout.

One problem was that he always gained a few pounds on surveillance when the stakeout became more like a steak-in. Even though he had eaten less than three hours prior, the *turble* fries had entered the round file, leaving only the cheeseburger, and Tender was feeling hunger pangs once more. He was famous for his bottomless pit, and he now felt like seafood, so he hopped over to Burke's for a crab cake sandwich, chips, and a Coke to go. Bea had taken Tender to the restaurant the initial time he had visited the Baltimore Inner Harbor area. With his meal on his wheels, he had asked for extra napkins so food or drink would not meet his cherished, rolled-and-pleated upholstery.

As he was enjoying the chow and staring at the hotel, he couldn't help thinking how the architectural design reminded him of the great Palmer House in Chicago and New York's Vanderbilt Hotel. He had once gone on a two-week tour of classic American hotels. He began to realize just how impressive the hotel designed by William L. Stoddart, built-in big-town "B-More" in 1928, appeared. Before he had gone on the excursion of exclusive guest houses, he had completed some study on the places where he would be staying, and he found that at the time it was constructed, the Lord Baltimore was the largest hotel in Maryland. Majestic.

With the nourishment, Tender's tools of observation were complete: the food; the binoculars and flash lamp, both stored in the glove compartment; and the reading material. He would bring a magazine or book, expecting an endurance race to see how long he could hold out before the spying effort either yielded some action or became futile. He had much experience in the process of repetition: eyeballs down to the printed matter, eyeballs up and in the direction of the those being watched, then repeat.

In one of his upward swings, he saw three figures coming out of the hotel laughing, each with an arm over another's shoulder and looking like a chain-link fence, obviously very happy. Tender picked up his field glasses to get a better angle. It was a trio of Baltimore Orioles: Mike Cuellar, Dave McNally, and Jim Palmer, pitchers, each winning a least twenty games in the 1970 regular season—more accurately, a combined total of 68 of the team's 108 checks in the win column that year. Tender surmised that they weren't celebrating their triumphs in that year's 162-game grueling schedule; instead, their joy was more likely a result of the team's 4-to-1 World Series victory over the Cincinnati Reds, affectionately known in the baseball world as the Big Red Machine. Very convincing. The triple play of winners in orange, black, and white moved merrily down Baltimore Street and out of sight.

Tender continued to examine a collector's item magazine that he had been able to place the winning bid on at an auction for a price he had always kept secret. It was an issue of *Graham's Magazine*, April 1841, with Poe's wonderful detective story that created the original fictional shamus, C. Auguste Dupin, "The Murders in the Rue Morgue." It has been said that Dupin was probably shaped after the real-life escapades of Francois Eugene Vidocq, a Paris investigator. Wonderful stuff.

Even though Tender's career path hadn't involved anything more creative than filling out reports and taking notes with his Montblanc, he admired great storytelling.

Thursday, 7:00 p.m. EST
Room 203
Lord Baltimore Hotel

A call came into the office of the Mechanix Limo Service, and Mechanix picked up the phone receiver.

"Mechanix's Limo, on-time, each time, never overtime. Can I help you?"

"Morris, this is Linguine. Can you come up to our room now, instead of later? We are ready to get going."

"Anything for my best clients. Be right there."

Mechanix dressed in his finest white-and-blue uniform; locked his agency door; headed down the hall; pushed the button for floor nineteen; and entered the elevator. He had already obtained new passports and fake IDs for the Sicilians—it would be the last he could get from the connection, his forger, an *artiste*, who had recently died unexpectedly in a car accident.

Thursday, 7:15 p.m. EST
Room 1939
Lord Baltimore Hotel

"Mechanix, can you do us a few more favors? Past that, we'll not need your services any further. You couldn't have been more dedicated to us if you were an actual member of the Vermicelli family. The don's illness has now become worse, and he wants to go back to the Old Country, Palermo, to die. The Festival of the Dead takes place on the second day of November. He wants to be there on the eve of that day when his dead uncle, Vito, returns from the grave, as is tradition, and gives Jonah his blessing to join him. Fagioli wants to be there to get some of the toys, sweets and cakes, and puppets of boiled sugar that the dead bring with them for the children of Palermo."

"I like the Martorana fruit the best," Fagioli said with an ear-to-no-ear grin on his face.

"What's Martorana fruit?" Mechanix asked. He had already arranged the trio's flight back to their homeland. He was not happy about the prospective lost revenue, but he always muted his emotions—a steadfast philosophy.

"It's an almond paste made into fruit shapes," Linguine responded.

"Better watch those calories, Fagioli. You don't have your boyish figure anymore. What are the favors? By the way, I have your new identities: Linguine now Tortelloni, Fagioli now Fettuccini, and Vermicelli now Don Ravioli."

"Great! First, we need you to contact your friend Perry at the Mason Travel Agency and see if we can move up our flight. Then we need you to take us to the airport," Linguine said.

"No problem, but Perry's on an assignment; his assistant, Miss Hale, can take care of the new bookings. What about the Lincoln?"

"I was getting to that. You can drive us in the Continental, and then we want you to sell it and send us the money, keeping a nice percentage for yourself. We've already closed out our savings account at the Maryland National Bank."

"*We will make you an offer you can't refuse*," Fagioli said.

"Puzo steal that line from Vermicelli too?" Mechanix questioned.

"No, that one was his," Linguine said. "Any problems with our requests?"

"None."

Thursday, 8:00 p.m. EST
Across from the Lord Baltimore Hotel
Tender's Stakeout

Tender put the spyglasses up to his face. Activity began to develop in the form of a golf foursome of men exiting the front doors of the Lord Baltimore. Darkness had snuck into the equation.

Through his binoculars, he saw the same three men that he had followed from Jake Venom's first funeral, but the fourth man he did not recognize. Standing under the marquee lights of the hotel, the man—dressed in a white uniform with royal blue patches and a baseball cap the same bright color—reminded Tender of a brawny Dough Boy, or more like a Dough Man. Could this be Morris Mechanix? Possibly. He couldn't read what was written on the patches of the man's uniform.

The white-and-blue fellow slid in behind the wheel of the vehicle and drove off with the other men sitting in the rear portion of the Lincoln. Tender cranked up his 289 Mustang and began to follow at a safe distance.

The Continental traveled toward St. Paul Street, turned right onto Light Street, and took another right to E. Conway. Tender knew they were heading toward I-295 South to merge onto the southern ramp of I-195. Maybe they were going to BWI, he surmised. But why? Perhaps making a getaway? From what?

About fifteen minutes later—this chauffeur driving much quicker than the one he had followed from Venom's first last rites, testing Tender's shadowing skills—the huge black luxury automobile took the BWI airport exit from Friendship Road, and Tender's suspicions were confirmed.

Once inside the airport, Tender followed the four to stops at customs, the currency-exchange counter, the duty-free shop, and eventually a British European Airways departure board. He observed that the white-and-blue-clothed fourth man was talking to the other three. Tender moved closer, positioning himself behind a wall so as not to be seen. He turned his left ear toward the conversation and gathered up his Montblanc pen and pad.

"Okay, Mr. Linguine, I'm sorry about this, but you all have to endure a layover in England before proceeding onto Italy. Your flight, number 2194, will land at the London Gatwick Airport."

Tender wrote down those details.

"Can we all sit together this time?" Fagioli said.

"Sorry, same situation as before: only seats of two together. But you'll be near a commode and in first class, row three this time."

"For my don."

Tender was finally able to read the emblem on the white-and-blue man's baseball hat: Mechanix Limo Service. "As I suspected," Tender whispered to himself. He felt that Mechanix may have a stronger relationship with these three men beyond just driving them to the airport. And what about all the associations in this whole state of killing affairs? The trio of Sicilian travelers in the photo with Jake Venom and in a meeting with Vincent March in LA. Vincent March in a business relationship with Jake Venom, and a too-casual connection with Vick Venom, the writer's widow. Fredric Price, an underling to Vincent March, is now dead. And finally, Jake Venom and King Bench, a possible cocaine alliance, and tragically, along with Price, three casualties of murder in this strange case. There were too many random events for Tender. His task was to tie it all together and establish some motives. He continued to listen.

"Mr. Linguine, you'll fly from London to Verona on Flight 2590, on which I found out, especially for Mister Fagioli's sake, that they will be serving asparagus with parmesan. Sorry, but Verona is the closest you'll be able to get to Palermo. I trust you have adequate transportation from there; unfortunately, I don't have any connections in Europe," Mechanix stated.

"It's taken care of. You just handle the selling of the Lincoln Continental. Do you know if they're providing fresh-grated Parmigiano-Reggiano with the asparagi al forno? It's the best Parmesan cheese."

"They use white or green *asparagi*?" Pasta E. Fagioli asked.

"And the Don wants to make sure that the airline is using freshly ground black pepper and extra virgin olive oil. Do you have that answer—oh, and he says to tell them to preheat the oven at 180 degrees centigrade."

"That translates to 356 degrees Fahrenheit; I do know about heating things," Mechanix responded. "But, as far as the other items, I didn't know you'd be that particular. Sorry, but I can only assume they know what they're doing."

The next thing Tender observed was several handshakes, so he quickly jotted "London/Verona 2590" and "Palermo" on the paper. He tried to copy the recipe he had just heard for Bea to use in the next Pillsbury side-dish bake-off that she might enter, but he wasn't able to get all the ingredients.

"Don Vermicelli just told me that Verona would be perfect; he said we can visit the Piazza dei Signori and see the statue of Dante, one of Italy's great writers. He wrote *La Divina Commedia,* the epic poem, you know. One of Vermicelli's heroes," Aldo Linguine interpreted.

"You mean Dante Alighieri's greatest work in three parts, 'Inferno,' 'Purgatorio,' and 'Paradiso,'" Mechanix said. "I own an illustration, which is on the wall at my place, with the poet standing in front of the mountain of Purgatory—hell on his right, heaven on his left. Doesn't one always go with the other?"

Tender thought, *Maybe, but one can only eternally exist in one or the other. The devil has experienced both, but there's no longer an apartment for him in the upstairs neighborhood.*

"Which was your favorite part?" Linguine asked Mechanix.

"'Inferno.' I've spread a little fire in my day. And I wrote a book once. Oh, well. You all had better get going; the plane is getting ready to fly into the clouds."

"As we leave you now, just remember what Christopher Morley, the American writer, and editor from Pennsylvania, once said …"

"I know, I know. 'No man is lonely while eating spaghetti; it requires too much attention.' *Arrivederci!*"

"Good, Morris, good," Linguine said.

The triad of Sicilians disappeared down the ramp, and Mechanix turned and walked toward the terminal.

Tender followed the Dough Man back to the Lord Baltimore.

CHAPTER 17

Thursday, 9:30 p.m. EST
Vick Venom's Home
Montpelier

"'How shall the burial rite be read? The solemn song be sung? The requiem for the loveliest dead, That ever died so young?'" Vicki Venom said.

"Yes, you really got everybody during the observance at the Poe house with those lines from E. A.'s poem, 'A Paean.' They all seem to have some sniffles. Guess Jake was really loved, Vick."

"Right."

"The Sicilians called earlier; they're on their way back to Sicily already," March said.

"Great. *The End* can now be put on the Fredric Price story. Guess you'll be hiring a new senior editor? One with a quieter mouth who can keep secrets 'huh,' as that stupid private investigator Tender always says."

"Wonder who killed poor Fredric?"

"Yes, I wonder? That is a mystery. What happened to the musical instrument we lent Fagioli to complete his job?" Vicki asked.

"It will be enjoying a nice dive to the bottom of the waters off Topanga Beach, as Linguine informed me."

"Excellent."

"When is the reading of your former husband's will?"

"Monday morning in our—or should I say, my—attorney's office."

"It was nice of Jake to also take out that extra two million's worth of life insurance on himself."

"I convinced him that it would leave me, along with the will, if he died before me, enough to live comfortably. And he always said he didn't want me to ever have to work. I have decided to enjoy my life. Use this money to do that, instead of existing like I did growing up. Let the cash fall where it may; we only pass by here once. Of course, I also suggested that he increase my policy too. Unfortunately, *someone* killed him first. More for me...us."

"Yes, that was rather unfortunate for Jake. And rather than hurt my business, his passing will help tremendously," March said with an evil smile. "Posthumous material of authors always does."

Mrs. Venom said, "No work until after our trip to Athens later, right?"

Mr. March responded, "You mean you want to go to Georgia and see all the Greek Revival buildings? Or do you want to go to the University of Georgia to take some classes?"

"Funny! You know I mean Athens, Greece. But, yes, there will no doubt be some afterschool, evening grades given out."

CHAPTER 18

Thursday, 10:45 p.m. PST
Room 203
Mechanix Limo Agency

Tender knocked on the door, hoping that Morris Mechanix would answer. Even though Tender had left his business card the previous Saturday, the limousine owner hadn't contacted him. And although it was pretty late on a school night, this business owner needn't worry about school bells anymore, so Tender didn't care what time it was. He needed some answers.

Mechanix came to the other side of the door. "Who's out there?"

"My name is Tim Tender. I left you my business card, huh?"

"Right, the private dick. What do you want with me? Do you realize what time it is?"

"I have your red-and-yellow business card that I found in Jake Venom's office, at his home in Montpelier."

The mahogany and frosted glass portal opened slowly. "Come in." Mechanix motioned with his right forefinger for Tender to sit on a green-colored leather sofa. Mechanix sat down in a chair upholstered the same as the couch. There was a glass-topped coffee table between the two pieces of furniture. Tender immediately noticed how Mechanix straightened up the magazines on the table; he had been getting ready to do it himself. He also observed how neat everything in the place was; if Tender didn't know better, he would've thought that he was in his own office.

"Want a Scotch? I only drink the Johnny Walker brand; I have some Red Label."

Tender immediately thought about the two glasses of cheap Scotch and bottle found in King Bench's apartment when he was killed. One had not been touched—maybe because it wasn't the right brand? "No, thanks. Got any orange soda, huh?"

"Look, you want any information out of me, you'd better have a drink with me, got it?"

Tender had to break a working cardinal rule and accept a drink, knowing if he didn't, he'd be wasting his time. He wasn't a Scotch fan, but he'd stomach it for the cause. "Okay, but just one. Where's your secretary?"

"One-man operation. Even if I had an assistant, she wouldn't be here this late; I'm not a taskmaster, just a driver. How do you want your drink?"

"Club soda and ice, huh."

"Sissy," Mechanix whispered to himself.

"What? I didn't hear you, huh?"

"Uh—nothing. You sure say 'huh' quite frequently. Did you know that?"

"Bad habit, trying to quit. Have you heard about Jake Venom's death a week ago Monday?"

"I read about it. So what?"

"Why would he have had your business card?"

"Haven't a clue. Maybe one of my clients gave it to him; I've run charters for lots of big shots, but not him. Never met the man. And I'm sure he wasn't the type to associate with somebody, not on his social scale. What benefit could he derive from it?"

"That's an interesting painting you have on your wall. What's it called? Little gruesome, isn't it?"

"*The Burial of Count Orgaz* by El Greco. The original was painted in 1586. If I had that one, I wouldn't be sitting here talking to you."

"Looks like a lot of big shots of the period attending."

"Is that what you came here to talk about?"

Tender took the picture of the three Sicilians and Jake Venom out of his jacket pocket. "Do you know these men in the photo standing with Mr. Venom?"

Without thinking, Mechanix responded, "No, I don't recognize them. Did you know that you dress like Philip Marlowe?"

Tender put the photo back in his coat for the moment. "Yes. Do you ever go skiing?"

"Sometimes I go up to the Catskills in southeast New York. I like to ski Slide Mountain, the highest peak."

"Did you know that the Catskill Mountains are in the region that Washington Irving used as a location for *Rip Van Winkle*?" Tender loved the interrogation game.

"Yes, I knew that."

"Do you wear a ski mask when you ski, huh?" Tender asked.

"No, I like the wind in my face; makes me feel alive. What does any of this have to do with anything?"

"Do you know a person called King Bench?"

"Do-don't recognize the name. Should I?"

"He was killed Saturday, like the way Jake Venom was done in. You didn't read about that in the *Sun*?"

"Sorry, didn't see that obituary."

"Probably because the story was only an inch long and buried in the back of the newspaper. Did you ever meet Vicki Venom, Jake's wife?"

"Man, you ask a lot of questions?"

"It's what I get paid for, huh."

Mechanix asked, "Who's paying you?"

"Mrs. Venom."

"Never met her either."

"Did you ever come in contact with Vincent March, Jake Venom's publisher at Premature Burial Publishing, or Fredric Price, the editor?"

"Never heard of them. Why are you asking me about all these people I don't know? Do you have any point to all these questions? You're starting to get on my nerves."

Tender pulled out the photo once more. "Why don't you look at this a little closer this time, see if you can't tell me the identity of these men."

It finally dawned on Mechanix that maybe this nosy sleuth had seen him leave the Lord Baltimore with Linguine, Vermicelli, and Fagioli: "Now that I study the photo, yes, these were three customers I took to the Dulles Airport."

"Where were they going?"

"Back to the old country; the oldest one is dying."

Tender immediately thought about extradition treaties. "What old country?"

"Ru—Russia. St. Petersburg, to be exact."

"Did you know that St. Petersburg, Florida, my hometown, was named after St. Petersburg, Russia? The story goes that Peter Demens, from Russia, and John C. Williams, from Detroit, flipped a coin to see who got to name the city. It's obvious who won the toss. Williams got the consolation prize and tagged the first hotel, The Detroit, which was ironically built by Demens.

"Marvelous. I don't care."

Maybe your three airport customers gave Venom your calling card." Tender couldn't believe how this guy was lying through his teeth. "Do you own a gun?"

"No, I hate them. Represents violence to me, and I'm not a violent person."

Tender decided that he had asked Mechanix enough questions for the time being and could always make a return engagement, which he would do with this canard-spouting driver. In Tender's justice-seeking brain, even though presently he couldn't think of any motive for Mechanix to have wanted to eliminate Venom, Bench, or Price, Mechanix's lying ways qualified him as a suspect.

Tender's next move would be to consult his BPD detective friend, Omaha, and compare notes. Then he'd visit with two characters who were increasingly, albeit slowly, becoming a little shady themselves. One of them was his possible temporary employer, a situation that he felt was probably on shaky ground.

Tender left the Lord Baltimore and headed toward Aunt Beryl's. Because of the lateness of the hour and the longer distance to his apartment, he had arranged to spend the night on the couch. Tiredness caused him not to notice the black limousine that was following him at a safe distance.

CHAPTER 19

Friday, 9:00 a.m. EST
Baltimore Police Department
Central District 1

Bea E. Hopkins was feeling worse and wouldn't be back at work yet. An infection might have developed, and she would need to see her dentist again.

Tender was at the station house conferring with Lieutenant Omaha.

"Okay, Rip, here's what I have so far, huh. The three Italians, probably Sicilians, having Palermo as a destination, knew Jake in some way, being in the photo op with him. They also had a meeting with Vincent March in LA, on the day that his senior editor, Mr. Price, was later found dead. Whether they know Mrs. Venom is a mystery. My guess is yes."

"And you say that you checked with the desk clerk at the Lord Baltimore, and they were staying in Room 1939?" Omaha said.

"Right, under the names of Linguine, Fagioli, and Vermicelli. Must be fictitious names. And the funny thing is that Morris Mechanix, the owner of the limousine agency whose business card, along with King's address, I found in Jake Venom's phone register, has his office at the same hotel and had serviced the trio before. Took them to BWI for the flights to England and Italy. He says that he never met Jake Venom, Mrs. Venom, March, or Price. What makes me curious about him is that when I originally showed him the photo of the Sicilians, he denied knowing them. Later, after I showed him the picture a second time, he suddenly remembered and offered some excuse for not looking at it closely enough the first time. He also lied about what airport he took them to and where they were going, but I have all the correct information if needed. I just can't figure a motive."

"Sounds like this boy has something to hide. I'll do a background check on him. And I'll check the passenger manifest to London Gatwick to see if the trio of Italians used those obviously made-up names. I'm still waiting for the reports from Lieutenant Sands in Santa Monica on Fredric Price and Vincent March; instead, he sent dossiers on Vincent Price and Fredric March. You know, he's not too smart; you weren't responsible for him not getting promoted."

"I know I wasn't responsible, but try telling him that. By the way, the Hollywood Vinnie Price was at Jake's funerals. Nice of him to make an appearance."

Omaha said, "I did get some information on Mr. Bench. Seems as though our drug connector was a Vietnam vet, dishonorably discharged. He and one of his buddies got drunk one night and beat up a local bar owner bad, in Thailand. Asian speakeasy owner later sank the eight ball on King, but the other courageous soldier was holding the little guy from behind, so the Asian couldn't describe him. King never scratched the cue ball on his cohort."

"Honor among thieves, so to speak, huh."

"What's better is that we found Jake's car behind the H. L. Mencken House on Hollins Street. Pretty well stripped. Strange, though: a monkey was living in it. Took the little guy down to the station, and some of the secretaries gave him the moniker Scopes for some reason."

"Interesting. H. L. was a one-time *Baltimore Sun* journalist and editor. That's a great brick row house, and it has an Italianate decorative scheme. Another writer's home? More symbolism, huh?"

"Starting to look that way. We finally found some fingerprints."

"Whose?"

"Mr. King Bench's."

"Curious."

"Not quite a royal flush, but starting to look at least like a pair," Omaha said.

"Yes, Jake and King sittin' in a tree—a dead tree."

"Sands told me Price was killed by the .22 short from a Beretta Minx, which they haven't found. We're going to compare all the bullets that were recovered. Their M.E. didn't find any snake venom in the system."

"Right, and the killer, or killers, in California used a Doubleday Dictionary instead of a Webster's like in the other cases."

"You think that makes a difference?"

"Yes. I think our Baltimore killer is compelled to do things the same way—a perfectionist, if you will," Tender said.

"Maybe I should make you a suspect. That sounds like you," Omaha said.

"I know; it's weird."

"What about the fact that he, or she, used a big, expensive dictionary on Jake and only a cheaper version paperback on King?"

"I think she, or he, is also a writer or someone close to a wordsmith, continually using the symbolism card, maybe feeling that Venom had the dockside value of the jumbo blue crab, whereas Bench only brought in clam-type money."

"Sounds like that stuff is rubbing off on you."

"Well, my brother Everett is a writer. Vincent March, according to Mrs. Venom, wrote a book called *Five Easy Steps to Publishing a Book.*"

"So what you're saying is that you think the Los Angeles criminal might be a copycat who just didn't have all the proper information? Maybe the Maryland mauler just wants us to think that it's separate assassins?"

"Possibly, but my conjecture, which at the moment is all that it remains, is there are different executioners."

"Got any ideas who the mimic could be?"

"I have a theory but need more info, and I think I know where to get it: at the lovely widow Venom's."

CHAPTER 20

Friday, 12:30 p.m. EST
Home of Vicki Venom
Montpelier

Tender knocked on the door of his employer, at least for the moment, thinking that after the line of questioning he was prepared to present her, he may have to continue his journey for justice fired. But his bottom line was always to see that the proper persons were held accountable, especially for a crime as horrendous as murder. He thought, in a moment of fancy, that if he was fired, maybe Erle Stanley Gardner's fictional detective, Paul Drake, might hire Tender at the Drake Detective Agency. *Quit daydreaming, Tender!*

Tender was beginning to believe that there might be some financial motives for the horror master's premature death in this now singly-owned Venom abode. The individual who answered his knock only slightly surprised Tender. He had suspicions that Vicki, aka Vick, might have a house guest.

"Oh, it's you, Tender," Vincent March said with disappointment evident in his voice.

"Fancy meeting you here, Mr. March."

"I extended him the invitation considering the hospitality he showed me in Santa Monica," Mrs. Venom said, sidestepping March from behind. "I didn't see any reason for him to stay in an unfriendly hotel by himself."

Except for the change of gender, Tender was sure he had heard that last statement before concerning these two, in California.

"If I'm to solve the death of your husband, I need to ask you both some questions, and some may be personal, huh?"

"Okay, but on one condition: you stop saying 'huh' so much," Vicki Venom said. She, Vincent March, and Tender walked into the living room and sat down, the lovely couple on an overstuffed sofa and Tender on a wooden rocker across from the fireplace that held Jake's photo memories on the mantel. Tender wasn't granted any offer of refreshment.

"I'll do my best. First, did either of you know Mr. King Bench, whose name, along with just his address but no phone number, I found in Jake's call pad?"

"No, but if this little person was—" Mrs. Venom started to say.

"Deceased human being!" Tender responded.

"Oh, right," she continued. "If Mr. Bench was Jake's drug connection, as you seem to infer, I knew nothing of it. I didn't even realize that Jake was doing drugs."

"You never noticed the rawness around his nose? He never acted out of the ordinary at any time, disoriented, or maybe a little too happy?"

"I occasionally noticed some rawness, but he picked his nose a lot. As for the other things you mention, if it happened, it took place behind the consistently closed doors of his creative chamber."

"That's quite a statement of alliteration. My brother told me about that term; he's a writer. Do you write, Vick—Vicki?"

"Don't be ridiculous."

For a moment, Tender got a flashback to a time when an uncontrollable finger used to drift toward his nostril, but he quickly broke the trance, remembering number seven of Todd's twelve-step program to break his twin's disgusting habit: *Don't dwell on the urge; erase it from your mind.* Tender was over it and back to the duty at hand. He knew he had other bad habits to break, especially his supreme wagering obsession, but he couldn't presently overwhelm himself with multiple cold turkeys.

"How about you, Mr. March? Ever notice anything unusual in Vicki's husband's manner, huh?"

"There he goes again, Vick—I mean Mrs. Venom—with that 'huh' stuff."

"Don't answer the question," Mrs. Venom said.

"Sorry, I'll rephrase it. How about you, Mr. March? Ever notice anything unusual in Vick's husband's manner?"

"That's better. No!"

"And you didn't know Bench either?"

"Never heard of him. But I'm very sorry about his untimely death." March reacted with a certain phony-baloney tone.

"Right. Do either of you enjoy skiing?"

March replied, "I've been known to haunt Vail and Steamboat Springs."

"Do you wear a ski mask when you ski?"

"Yes. It keeps the cold wind off my face. Why?"

"What color is it?"

"The wind?"

"The mask, smart guy."

"I usually wear yellow—gives me a bright feeling."

"How about you, Mrs. Venom?"

"Mrs. Venom isn't an avid skier; she just likes to—"

"No! I don't ski. Is that important?" Vicki asked.

She gave March a mean-spirited glance, and Tender caught it.

"Not really," Tender said. "Did I mention that the Baltimore Police found your dearly departed's Jaguar behind the H. L. Mencken home?"

"Great. Can I get it back?"

"Probably not for a while; it's evidence. Besides, what's left of it couldn't pass for an automobile. A real shame to do that to such a fantastic piece of machinery."

"Did the police find any clues in the Jag?" Vincent March said.

"Mr. King Bench's fingerprints, along with Jake's and Mrs. Venom's, were located in and on the car. Mrs. Venom, you can't offer any explanation for Mr. Bench's fingerprints on your husband's Jaguar?"

"None. Does Lieutenant Omaha consider him a possible suspect in my ex-husband's killing?"

Tender thought, *Ex-husband? So soon?* "Yes, I'm sure he would've been, right up until the time King was found dead."

"Oh, right. I suppose that's true," Venom said.

"One way to get off the suspect list," March added.

"Amusing, Mr. March, very entertaining," Tender said, feeling an attack of nausea coming on.

"Sorry, couldn't resist."

Tender said, "Did your husband leave a will, Mrs. Venom?"

"He did. Jake loved me very much and wanted to make sure that I was taken care of in case he passed on before me."

"Mr. March, while in Los Angeles, I had a little chat with your administrative assistant, Hesta Perrine, and she said that you've had to suffer some layoffs at Premature Burial. Money problems at the publishing house?"

"As you know, Mr. Tender, we never received Jake's latest manuscript. He hadn't had a bestseller in quite a spell, but the company is fine, believe me. Besides, I'm presently negotiating with a new writer. Price read a piece that this writer had sent to a magazine called *Comics Review* when he was only eighteen. Marvelous stuff, Price had advised. Poor Fredric. I think that this writer could become our main horse, replace Jake, stay in it for the long run, and bring us back to the prominence we once enjoyed. Says he has a story, an instant million-plus seller, about a girl exacting revenge on her high school classmates for bullying her; she has the power to move things without touching them."

"Telekinesis," Tender noted.

"Right. You seem very knowledgeable," March said.

"I read. Do you have any idea why someone would have wanted to kill your senior editor?"

"Haven't the foggiest. Vick and I both had alibis."

Vicki Venom was getting impatient. "Vincent! I'm sure that this PI already knows that. Do you have any more questions, Mr. Tender? We have lunch reservations downtown at Tio Pepe's?"

"Mrs. Venom and I are going to split some of Tio Pepe's delicious paella for two. She's treating me, and I never pass up a great meal, especially one that comes with no weight loss from my wallet. Although I probably should leave the tip."

"Big of you. Most meals are market price, you know? Just one more question for now." Tender took out the photo that had become his constant companion. "Mrs. Venom, did you know the three men in the picture with your husband, and if so, how well did you know them? Mr. March had a meeting with them about something in LA, but what about your relationship with them?"

"Those men came here once seeking counsel from Jake about what to do about the older one's manuscript. They said Mario Puzo had stolen some of his ideas. Jake referred them to Vincent to see if he could help; that's the only time I've ever even seen them. We exchanged a few courtesies when they were here, and I took this photograph. Jake asked me to. He had always liked to have his picture taken with other people, especially those he felt might, presently or in the future, show up in the headlines. Even though my ex-husband was a very famous person, he was still a name-dropper."

"Vick, you didn't tell me you met them in Baltimore," March said.

"Quiet, Vincent!"

There was that "ex-husband" reference again. Tender thought that considering Jake had only been scattered to rest the day before, it was a little cold. Presently, he decided not to hit the lovely couple with the interrogation that might cause him to lose his present employment; those queries involved the seemingly cozy relationship that Vick and Vincent had developed since Jake Venom had died. Or had this unlikely union been brought to fruition long before the terror author began his postmortem writing?

As Tender stood up to vacate the premises, his eyes, acting conspiratorially, fixed on the photo on the mantel of Jake and the Oriole Robinsons, looking beyond the trio and noticing the bright red truck and the words "On Time." While viewing the picture for a second time, something finally dawned on him. He walked out the front door of the home of widow Venom, fast-paced down the driveway, reached into the open window of his Mustang, and pulled out the Morris Mechanix Limo Agency business card from his glove compartment. That was it: part of the company slogan. Why would Mechanix lie, saying that he had never met Jake Venom? He did say he had serviced several stars, so maybe he forgot, but Tender didn't think so. Another interview was warranted. First, he needed to retrieve that picture. As he was heading back toward the house, he noticed the curtains drawn in the windows to the left of the front door. Two individuals were standing in the living room hugging each other, lovey-dovey style.

He quietly knocked and said that it would help the case to have the photo in question in his possession for a while. His request was granted without hesitation. Was their instant cooperation possibly a calculation to get rid of him and attend to more personal matters? Tender didn't make mention or use any body language to reveal his spontaneous sighting of the alleged lovebirds.

His next move was to update, and be updated by, Omaha.

CHAPTER 21

Friday, 3:00 p.m. EST
Baltimore Police Department
Central District 1

"We received the dollars-and-cents registers on Vincent March and Fredric Price from Lt. Sands," Omaha told Tender.

"Anything interesting, huh?"

"Seems as though Mr. March's business, Premature Burial Publishing, may be on the way to its last rites. The company has been in Chapter 11 for some time."

"Financial reorganization. Funny, he didn't mention that when I recently talked to him and Vick, as he refers to her."

"That's a cute pet name."

"My sentiments exactly," Tender said.

"Sands says that according to Hesta Perrine, Price's position was soon to be eliminated. Apparently, he had a huge salary."

"Bumping him off is kind of a harsh way to get rid of a paycheck; he must have had something more severe on the boss, considering the Doubleday Dictionary mentioned blackmail."

Omaha said, "I would think so. Here's another juicy tidbit: our investigation revealed a very recent two-million-dollar increase in Jake Venom's life insurance policy, drawn up through a local subsidiary of Lloyd's of London."

"She's not as dumb as I originally presumed her to be."

"Good actress."

"A real Betty Joan Perske."

"Who?"

"That's the name Lauren Bacall was born with," Tender said.

"How do you know these things?" Omaha asked.

"I spent a lot of time in cinema houses and libraries when I was younger."

"Here are some other little gems of information. Guess what your Mister Morris Mechanix did before becoming a limousine owner? He spent a couple of years in Haight-Ashbury, but before that, he attended the University of Maine at Orono, trying to get an English degree. Before he was able to complete it, he dropped out a semester, was drafted, and was shipped to the jungles of Vietnam. All that preceded his San Franciscan-flower-in-your-hair days. And get this: he was in the same outfit as Mister King Bench."

"The brave soldier who got away, huh? Did you get a home address on him? Probably find some interesting things there."

"Be my guess too. No, the only address we could come up with was the same one as his business, at the Lord Baltimore."

"Curious. He denied knowing King—said he didn't recognize the name," Tender said.

"I'd say it would be easier to get four aces in a game of Five-Card Stud than not knowing the name of somebody in your outfit, especially two who made it back and settled in the same town," Omaha said.

"Probably less chance than a filly winning the Triple Crown."

"Ever happen?"

"Never."

"By the way, the three Sicilians didn't use those names on the tickets that you mentioned. There were three guys listed by the names of Tortelloni, Fettuccini, and Ravioli. The funny thing, though, is Fettuccini's seat was empty—never used."

"Maybe Linguine, Fagioli, and Vermicelli are names that are real, not fake, as we had presumed. I think they're involved in this whole deal somehow."

"If they turn out to be conspirators or actual participants in a murder or murders, I don't think extraditions would be a problem."

"*Malum in se* crimes, huh?"

"Yes, 'acts criminal by their very nature.' You've done your homework."

"I read, *grazie*," Tender said.

"*Si*, but we need more concrete evidence to make any arrests. Although, it seems as though we're getting some definite possibilities here. One more thing: Sergeant Small, in his investigation around King's neighborhood, may have found a witness who noticed a vehicle—a truck, he thought—driving out of the back alley behind King's place shortly after you discovered the body. Don't know how credible he is, though."

"Did the witness notice the color?"

"Said it was definitely green, red, or blue."

"Real sure of himself, huh? *Ciao,* Rip."

"*Arrivederci*, PI."

CHAPTER 22

Saturday, 11:00 a.m. EST
Aunt Beryl's Pad

Tender had been at Aunt Beryl's most of the morning trying to comfort Bea, who was in obvious agony. Dr. Wunderman, the remarkable tooth man, was going to take a look at her infection and recommend a treatment to hopefully alleviate the pain. Beryl would drive Tender's girl in her 1968 gold Cadillac Eldorado, which had just come back from being repaired.

As the two ladies left, Tender started toward downtown, hoping to catch his limo-driving suspect at his office. Mr. Mechanix had a lot of explaining to do. There were untruths on the surface that needed cleaning up, chief among them denying that he had ever crossed paths with Jake Venom or King Bench, unfortunate victims of some homicidal maniacs' reign of Baltimore terror. Was it also conceivable, but not likely in Tender's estimation, that the killer could be a coast-to-coast slayer, ending the life prematurely of poor Fredric Price, whose body was discovered on the rocks in California?

CHAPTER 23

Saturday, 2:45 p.m. EST
Lord Baltimore Hotel
Room 1939

Vincent March stopped searching when he heard a knock at the door. He had taken the room under an assumed name. Vick was running late. She had told him that she would meet him there. He pulled back the portal, and a large man dressed in a brown leisure suit, also wearing brown gloves and a brown fedora, stood in the doorway.

"What are you do—" March uttered when a blackjack struck him on top of the head, instantly knocking him unconscious. It was a powerful blow. Then a shot rang out.

Saturday, 3:45 p.m. EST
Lord Baltimore Hotel
Room 203

Tender was just about to leave the front of the Mechanix Limousine Agency when he heard the elevator door open. Mechanix stepped out, and a deep frown quickly developed on the ex-vet's face as he noticed PI Tender. Mechanix walked slowly down the hall toward him decked in his white-and-royal-blue uniform. Tender knew Mechanix wouldn't be especially thrilled to see him. He didn't care.

Suddenly, Tender heard a single siren from the street. He and his seemingly-without-a-motive suspect entered the office, and Mechanix moved to open the window behind his desk. Tender followed. Baltimore police cars, a WBAL News van, and a coroner's wagon were down on the pavement below.

Tender also recognized a classic Edsel parked on the scene. Omaha was just entering the building.

"I'm sorry, Mr. Mechanix. I'll have to get with you later."

"Don't put yourself out on my account." Mechanix closed and relocked the window and the office door after Tender exited.

Saturday, 4:00 p.m. EST
Lord Baltimore Hotel
Room 1939

"I guess we can take Vincent March off the suspect list, PI?" Lt. Omaha said. "Last hand played."

"Can I see the body?"

"Sure."

The zipper on the black bag was pulled back, and Tender immediately noticed the small hole between the eyes. "Twenty-two short, I'll bet?"

"Probably a good wager."

"Raise ya and say snake venom in the system."

"Pot's right, but that hand hasn't been played yet. M.E. is up next."

"Any witnesses, anybody hear anything?"

"Guy delivering room service down the hall heard what he thought was a firecracker. Thought it might be some kids playing games, so after getting rid of his customer's food and beverage, he rushed downstairs to the lobby to tell the supervisor. Turns out that the front desk person noticed a large man walking briskly down a side hall toward an exit. Said he glanced at him because of the brown leisure suit he was wearing."

"Eyeball his face, huh?"

"No, the attendant said he had a brown fedora, the brim pulled down to cover most of his face."

"Mrs. Venom said that she and Mr. March were coming down here yesterday to lunch at Tio Pepe's. Anybody happen to see her around? I think she's going to be very upset when she finds out about this."

"Nobody mentioned anyone of her description."

Tender mused, "Curious. Room 1939 was the one the Sicilians stayed in."

Omaha added, "Another peculiar thing: The room wasn't registered to Vincent March but Fredric Price."

"Some sort of a sick joke? Not funny. I'll be back in a minute. I'm going to call Mrs. Venom and give her the bad news."

"I guess she'll need to ID the body; she knew him better than anybody around here, right?"

"I think so. I'll tell her to come down to the coroner's office later." Tender left and shortly came back. "She's not home or just not answering."

"Why wouldn't she pick up?" said Omaha.

"Probably thinks it's me; I think she's going to boot me off the case. Is that another Webster's Dictionary on his right arm?"

"No, it's a Doubleday."

"Highlighted words, huh?" Tender said.

"Says, 'The Harlequin gets what is coming to him.' Think the Pacific killer has made his way to the Atlantic?"

"In the commedia dell'arte theater, Arlecchino, sometimes called Harlequin, was a clownish valet, not caring about right or wrong and always looking for food and female companionship. A characterization that resembles March, I think."

"Man, you have too much time on your hands," said Omaha.

"With this killer using symbolism, maybe the same criminal is working both coasts."

"Sounds like we might be back behind the eight ball again. I'll let you know the results of the M.E.'s findings."

"When you're done here, could you do me a favor?"

"Sure."

"I need you to switch cars with me later. Here is my plan."

CHAPTER 24

Saturday, 4:45 p.m. EST
Lord Baltimore Hotel
Gift Shop/Lobby

Tender stopped by the hotel gift shop to buy some mints—actually, two rolls; his present package contained only one Breath Saver. Tender always tried to keep a backup of items that he felt that he didn't want to run out of. He also wanted to stop by the front desk and talk to the identifier of the brown-suited man to see if there was anything that he failed to tell the police.

"Good afternoon, sir, my name is Tim Tender, I'm a private investigator working on the Jake Venom case. Are you familiar with it, huh?"

"Yes. It's too bad—a great writer, and wonderful book, *Tender Nightmare.* I never figured out that the Hitler worm was inside the—"

"Maybe we can talk about the book review later. Your name is, huh?"

"No, not 'huh.' Hector Holmes."

"Hector—Puerto Rican, correct?" Tender said.

"I know, not British, but my parents loved reading about the consulting private detective, Sherlock."

"Is there anything, Mr. Holmes, that you can remember other than what you told the Baltimore PD? Anything at all, no matter how insignificant you might feel it is, huh?

"No, I don't believe so."

"Take your time. Focus on the head of the brown-suited man. You said the hat was pulled down?"

"Right, I couldn't see his face—wait, I was concentrating on trying to see his face, and now I remember. He turned once, and the right side of his head was missing the ear, just a good-sized hole there."

Tender pulled out the photograph of the three Sicilians with Jake Venom and showed it to the desk clerk. The biggest one, Pasta E. Fagioli, alias Fettuccini, was the man Holmes picked as matching closest to the person that had left through the hallway.

Tender asked the desk clerk if he could use the desk phone. Yes. He called up to room 1939 and told Omaha of the discovery. He mentioned to the lieutenant that he might want to have some officers go over to BWI in case the man in the brown leisure suit was trying to leave the country this time. He also told Omaha that the cops could stop by the lobby and get the picture of the Sicilians. Omaha told Tender that he would send somebody to Dulles, just in case. Great idea, Tender felt.

"Holmes, that could be important in later identifying him. Thanks for your help. I may want to talk to you in the future."

"You'd better do it soon; I'm leaving for vacation tomorrow."

"Oh? Where are you vacationing, Holmes?"

"Have you ever been to Baker Street? It's wonderful."

"Ah, London, your namesakes' neighborhood. Will you still go if it becomes inconvenient?"

"Convenient or not, I will go all the same!"

Saturday, 5:15 p.m. EST
Lord Baltimore Hotel
Room 203

Tender knocked on Mechanix's door for a second time that afternoon. The limo driver answered with a straight Scotch on ice in hand—looked like a double to Tender.

"Guess you needed a drink?" Tender questioned.

"I don't ever need one. Just like to have one when I feel like it. I poured you one with club soda, wimp, I figured you'd be back. What was all the commotion?"

"You don't know, huh?"

"How could I?"

"Mr. Vincent March, whom I asked you about before, has been killed in room 1939. Isn't that the room that was recently occupied by the clients that you drove to Dulles, according to you, and who were flying to St. Petersburg, Russia?"

"Now that you mention it, I believe that was their room. Quite a coincidence."

"Yes, quite," Tender said.

"What do you want?"

"Where had you been when I saw you come out of the elevator?"

"Uh—I was at the movies," Mechanix said.

"You wear your uniform to the movies?"

"Never know when or where you might get an unexpected fare," Mechanix said.

"What movie did you see, huh?"

"If you must know, I—I saw—uh, um, *The Great Escape*, where they show those older first-run movies."

"Terrific flick. Paul Newman was great in that, wasn't he?" said Tender.

"Right, he's a great actor."

"How 'bout when Paul's character tried to escape by flying over the barbwire fence on a motorcycle?"

"Yes, that was an exciting scene. Newman must know a bunch about bikes."

Tender couldn't believe it: this guy was lying again. If he had seen *The Great Escape*, he would know that Steve McQueen played that part, not entirely using a stunt double except for the famous jump scene, which was handled by Bud Ekins, a real pro. *Joanne Woodward's husband wasn't even in that movie, dummy.*

"Yes, what a triumph for Mr. Newman. Maybe he didn't even use a stunt double?"

"I don't think he did," Mechanix said.

Tender thought, Either this guy has something serious to hide, or he's a habitual liar and can't help himself. He noticed a brown fedora hanging on a hat rack behind a file cabinet.

"Is that your brown fedora?" PI Tender loved the part of his chosen field that dealt with grilling. He knew that if enough questions were presented in such a way, especially to the guilty, eventually the cat—or at least a kitten—would come strolling out of the bag.

"No, it belongs to one of my clients, who wants me to UPS it to him," Mechanix said.

"Ups?"

"UPS, United Parcel Service. I thought you were a detective."

"Belong to one of the Italian trio, possibly?"

"No, another customer. No one you would know."

"You like to protect your clients, huh?"

"Good business practice."

"Right."

Tender continued to survey the room without moving his head; he had astounding peripheral vision. He felt Mechanix didn't have a clue.

There was a cot under a window covered by a blanket that touched the floor—on it was a likeness of Jim Morrison. It was close to a wooden door that led to another room. A hot plate and small refrigerator were located close to the mahogany portal. Back in St. Petersburg, Tender's dear friend Dink Playlen had taught him how to recognize different types of wood.

"What's in the other room?" he asked.

"If it's any of your business, a bathroom."

"Do you have a home address?"

"N-no, I live here."

"You mean in one of the hotel rooms, huh?"

"No, here, right here. Why do you think I have all this stuff in the office that you've been studying without shifting your head?"

"Can I use the restroom? 'Doody' Calls."

"You consider relieving yourself a duty?"

"Not d-u-t-y but do-o-d-y. You know, a number two."

"Oh, man. No more, please. Go ahead."

In the bathroom, there was a shower stall with a psychedelic-colored curtain, a toilet with a lid cover painted the same colors, a one-spigot sink, and a mirrored medicine cabinet. On the back of the door, hung uniforms identical to the one Mechanix was presently wearing, but it was the only type of clothing evident. Could this be the only form of dress Mechanix wore? Did he simply add a tie to the outfit when he needed to dress up? Tender doubted it. He must have personal attire somewhere else.

In the medicine cabinet was a red toothbrush, a tube of Gleem fluoride with half the paste squeezed out, and a full, unopened bottle of Listerine mouthwash. No lotions, cologne, or shaving cream.

Another conspicuously missing thing was deodorant—not even an empty one in the small garbage can next to the crapper. Unless Mechanix thought that body odor—which was not at all apparent when Tender entered the office—was a turn-on, this was confirmation Mechanix had put the smelly stuff on at his residence that day, not this so-called working and living arrangement.

He noticed a can of air freshener on the windowsill, grabbed it, flushed the toilet, and gave the room a spray to hide the fact that he hadn't left a biological odor. He had done a number one, which, because of his bladder problem, always made evidence-seeking bathroom trips legit, but he hadn't been in there long enough for a number two.

Tender decided to delay any further questioning of Mechanix and instead put his plan into effect. Like Sherlock Holmes, living on in many brilliant stories of observation, deduction, and knowledge penned by Sir Arthur Conan Doyle, would say, "The plot thickens."

"Mr. Mechanix, I'm sorry, but we'll have to continue this conversation later."

"As I said before, no need to go out of your way for little old me. Just for your info—"

"All you need to say is FYI. I will understand what you m—"

"Can I please continue?"

"Of, course," Tender said.

"FYI, I will be leaving here around 8:00 p.m., so don't come back then."

"Perfect."

CHAPTER 25

Saturday, 8:05 p.m. EST
Lord Baltimore Parking Area
Plan A

Mechanix was pulling away from the hotel driving the Lincoln Continental stretch still owned by the Sicilians. He drove east on West Baltimore and immediately saw in his passenger's side mirror that a black with a white convertible top, 1965 Mustang was following him.

Did this private eye think he was that dumb? Mechanix wanted to tell Tender that he needed to hone his tailing skills—this was too obvious. Mechanix knew a few choice truths that Tender wasn't aware of: first, he knew the kind of classic car that Tender owned and drove; second, he knew that Tender had some connection to a row home where two women lived, close to the section in the same neighborhood as his.

Because of his profession, Mechanix knew the city like the front and back of his hand and felt his pursuer didn't stand a chance. It was true, Mechanix thought, what Sherlock Holmes often said to Dr. Watson: "The game is afoot." One reason he enjoyed the unofficial detective of Doyle's books was that he had some of the same controllable vices as Mechanix. He pressed the accelerator.

He moved onto E. Monument Street; up Edison Highway, past some dentist's office; over to Gray Street and E. Eager; and finally, upon completing the circle, lost Tender on Orleans Street. Victory! He then continued toward his home in Armistead.

Private Investigator Tender, in Lieutenant Omaha's champagne-colored Edsel, picked up the black Lincoln limousine as it took a left on Orleans. In his Mustang tracking sting, his Ford vehicle, driven by Omaha, hung a right on the opposite stretch of paved asphalt, completing Tender's original part of the two-part plan.

Tender knew he had to learn Mechanix's address and later search his quarters in hopes of uncovering clues that would lead to a killer. Part A of his blueprint was working perfectly.

What surprised Tender was that Mechanix resided in the identical section of Baltimore as his beloved Bea and her adored Aunt Beryl, the celebrated Gardens.

CHAPTER 26

Monday, 9:53 a.m. EST
Lord Baltimore Hotel
Part B

Mechanix was motoring in the Sicilian's dark stretch limo toward Ellicott City and St. Johns Lane to retrieve a party-of-two flying United Airlines to Clearwater Beach, Florida, for a last-minute getaway. He had put an advertisement in the classified section of *The Baltimore Sun* offering the Continental for sale but had yet to receive any offers. He thought it would be a nice touch to use the big black limousine instead of the smaller red one. He felt the clients would be more impressed.

The Ellicott City pickup was in Howard County, Maryland, west of Baltimore proper. The community is best known as the home of the United States' oldest surviving passenger train station, the B&O, since 1830. Mechanix loved visiting the town, mostly because of its historic value.

His customers' flight was scheduled at 12:23 in the afternoon, and his steadfast rule was to reserve pick up times at least two hours in advance to give the patrons ample time to check their baggage; obtain the gate number; visit the many marvelous amenities offered by BWI; and rest their rears in the seats assigned without ever feeling rushed. All this for the affordable price of thirty dollars—fifteen each. "Try taking a taxi for that price," he always told his customers when they had the gumption to question the charge.

This was a reservation phoned into his office around 5:45 p.m. on Saturday, but he had nothing pressing on the fire for Monday, so he gladly took the run. A Mr. and Mrs. Linc Nebraska had called for the booking.

Monday, 10:23 a.m. EST
Morris Mechanix's Place
Armistead Gardens

Using his special entry skills, Private Eye Tender was invading the row home of his lying suspect hoping to find something, anything, that could incriminate the transfer-business proprietor in any one of the murder cases that seemed to be tied together in some manner. In Tender's opinion, no one fabricates as much as Mechanix without something serious to conceal.

Part B of the Tender-Omaha scheme to get Mechanix back on the road was falling into place nicely. Lieutenant Omaha and one of the Baltimore Police Department's fine female detectives, J. Marple, were posing undercover as the Nebraskas. Omaha had vouchered the payment for the ride, expensing it to the Jake Venom and King Bench investigations. They would make sure that Tender was afforded a sufficient session to complete the search at Mechanix's.

The first thing Tender saw was the ominous painting of Dante at the *Mountain of Purgatory.*

"This guy has some strange taste in art," Tender said to the empty room. He plunged into the hunt. He looked and searched, searched and looked in every crevice of the bungalow: the screened-in front porch (he kept low while out there to avoid detection), kitchen, living room, up the stairs to the top floor, into the two bedrooms, and finally the full bathroom. He found nothing that would frame a chargeable web around Mechanix. He did see a stick of deodorant, though.

He went back downstairs and sat down on a love seat made from the same green-leather material used on the furniture in the limousine agency's office. Tender stared at the paneled walls made of honey maple for what seemed like an eternity. The rows of yellowish-brown wood were in sections, each about four feet wide. Then he saw it. One segment was a lighter shade than the other amber ones.

He took out his Swiss army knife—the one with the red plastic handle used by the Swiss military as opposed to the anodized aluminum grips most people possessed—and pulled out the screwdriver blade. Tender began to loosen the wood and, lo and behold, the process revealed an empty space between that part of the paneling and a plaster wall.

The items that Tender discovered almost made his heart jump away from its aortic and pulmonary arteries: two stacks of Webster's dictionaries, one softback, the other hardback, side-by-side, with the *pistola résistance* at the top of the more expensive reference pile: a revolver and its holster—.22 Beretta Minx, Tender noted. On the peak of the paperback mountain was an opened box of plastic surgical gloves—supplying an explanation for the fruitless dustings for fingerprints at the murder scenes.

Further investigation in the shadowy part of the crevice revealed an aquarium, but not a tank containing any salt or freshwater or colored gravel. Nor were there any fish toys, little men in diver's suits, or small caves. No plants either. What was in there were pieces of wood shavings and a dead rat. Tender bet himself that the rodent was chock full of snake venom. Animal autopsy? Next to the fish alias viper reservoir sat a covered basket, the kind snake charmers use.

Tender backed away from the wooden wall, and the private eye eyed a cover over a piece of equipment that was sitting on a tiny table in front of a window that faced the Fox Mansion—a place he had, on many occasions, danced the night away with his disco queen girl, Bea.

Why hadn't this registered before? He walked to the case, and under it was an old Remington typewriter. He immediately took a piece of paper, rolled it into the machine, pressed the Caps Lock key, and typed, "WOODSTOCK." As he had suspected, the word that symbolized the revolutionary rock festival of 1969 inked the parchment as "WQQDSTQCK."

There were *Q*s instead of the proper *O*s.

Tender instantly knew why Jake Venom, famous—or starting to look more like infamous—for *his* horror words was killed.

And these findings were enough solid evidence to bring Mechanix, a one-man limousine company owner, straight to the suspect summit. But where were the runaway rough draft, yellow ski mask, and cobras?

Monday, 10:23 a.m. EST
Ellicott City

Mechanix knocked on the door of the two-story house at St. Johns Lane. No one answered. He rang the doorbell. Nothing. He hit the portal three times in succession with a fist-clenched hand. No luck. He then walked around the right side of the home, hung a left in front of the detached garage to the back area, and saw a set of sliding glass doors. He banged on them without success. He yelled out, "Is anybody here? Mr. and Mrs. Nebraska, it's Mechanix Limo Company here to take you to the airport."

He was getting even more irritated than he already was as a result of being cut off while coming off the US-29S ramp by an ugly Edsel. He gave the other driver, a woman, the finger—seemingly his favorite reaction in traffic—and couldn't believe she would own such a dog for an automobile.

What Mechanix didn't realize at that precise moment—and what Tender didn't know, because there was no time to contact them—was that the Nebraskas, alias Lt. Omaha and Det. J. Marple had to leave unexpectedly because Marple's son had had an accident at No. 234 Elementary.

Mechanix went back to the Continental, where it was warm, and waited. His policy was to stay fifteen minutes beyond the actual pickup time just in case the customers went to the store or were in the shower and had not heard his knocks—or something.

Mechanix's grace period passed, and he returned to the front patio—still no luck. Now he was incensed. These imbeciles probably decided to take other means—a relative or friend making a last-minute decision to transport the Nebraskas. This was fine. The problem arose when the passengers didn't have enough courtesy to call the office and cancel. That drove Mechanix crazy!

Mechanix noticed a semi-stained-glass window to the left running the same length as the door. Through parts of it, the inside of the residence could be seen.

Then he saw it: a Baltimore Police cap on the wall with other types of hats, most of the car-racing and classic vehicle variety. That was it. He'd been buffaloed, and he had a feeling that the stupid private investigator was behind the whole bamboozle. Mechanix knew what he had to do and had the perfect, portable piece of equipment—hidden in his office—to handle the job.

When he turned over the ignition of the Sicilians' long auto, the radio was blaring the lyrics "There's something happening here, But what it is ain't exactly clear" from the classic song, "For What It's Worth" by Buffalo Springfield.

Mechanix said to himself, "It's becoming clearer by the minute and somebody's going to pay, huh!" He tuned his ears again to what was coming out of the music machine.

"Paranoia strikes deep, Into your life it will creep, It starts when you're always afraid, Step out of line, the men come and take you away."

Mechanix forcefully turned off the tune player and floored the gas pedal.

CHAPTER 27

Monday, 11:30 a.m. EST
The Mechanix Row Home

After Tender, from a drugstore phone box, had contacted him about the gems of revelation at Mechanix's place, Lieutenant Omaha obtained an arrest warrant for one Morris Mechanix for the crime of murder in the first degree.

Tender learned from Omaha that after the third day of staking out Baltimore–Washington International disguised as skycaps— Omaha's idea—Sergeant Small and Detective Broadly captured the brown leisure-suited man with the missing ear. And pleasingly, much to everyone's surprise, a shocking development had developed: not only did Fagioli fall into their paws, but an additional shady character dropped in: Vicki, ex-Mrs. Jake Venom. She was attempting to leave the country with the Pasta man. The second .22 semiautomatic was discovered in a secret compartment of Fagioli's instrument case under an actual violin—a classic Stradivarius.

They were both in custody at Central One headquarters. The criminal suspects were all starting to "lay down their poker hands," as Omaha might say. Tender dearly wanted to talk to the widow of Jake Venom. Possibly, later.

Now, the two law-seeking friends needed to wait, Tender at Mechanix's and Omaha at the Lord Baltimore, for the limousine driver to show after the prearranged wild goose chase. Omaha advised Tender about the Marple predicament—the reason for the quick exit from Tender's plan—and that J. Marple's son would be fine. He also said that he would send out an officer to collect the overwhelming evidence at Mechanix's place.

Unfortunately, Mechanix had advanced a spontaneous strategy far from the scheme that Tender and Omaha had hoped he would follow.

CHAPTER 28

Monday, 11:35 a.m. EST
Aunt Beryl's Row Home

The business end of a light, hand-held flamethrower was pointed right at Bea E. Hopkins and her favorite aunt, Beryl. The opposite end was connected at the handle with Mechanix's sizeable paws.

The weekend and Dr. Wunderman's miracle remedy had allowed Bea to recover from her quadruple extractions, and she was now able to talk. "How did you know where this home is?"

"You can thank that idiot investigator, Tender. I followed him here late last Thursday. What is he, your boyfriend or something?" Mechanix asked.

"They're engaged, you moron," Aunt Beryl added.

"That's excellent, more than I could've hoped for."

"You shadowed my Timster? What do you want with us?" Bea E. said.

"Shadowed? Where did you come up with that term?" Mechanix said.

"I just finished *The Maltese Falcon* by Dashiell Hammett. What's it to you? What are you going to do with us?"

Aunt Beryl was nervous and started rolling some Bull Durham tobacco into a sheet of cigarette paper.

"Oh, you two are just a little insurance, aces in the hole, so to speak. I think your fiancé—by the way, when are you getting hitched?"

"None of your business, creep," Beryl said.

"Couple of feisty broads. I like tough women. But I'm tough too, and I have the upper hand. So, pipe down.

"As I was saying, I think your fiancé got one over on me— believe me, a difficult thing to do. And he's probably discovered enough evidence by now to have my pretty posterior strapped into two thousand volts of electric current for the killings of Mister Big Shot, so-called writer, or should I say ex-writer, Jake Venom, and that lowlife, King Bench."

"Pretty posterior? I believe you mean Fat Butt," Bea E. said with forcefulness. "Tender's suspicions about you weren't unfounded."

"Did you snuff out all those innocent people?" Aunt Beryl asked.

"Innocent! Innocent! There wasn't anything moral about any of them. What cave of purity have you been hibernating in? Besides, I didn't kill all of them, only dear Jake and that scum, Bench."

Bea responded, "If you didn't do away with Fredric Price and Vincent March, then who did?"

Mechanix said, "Why don't you ask your boyfriend? He seems to know everything. Genius, I guess you think. Huh?"

Aunt Beryl chimed in. "At least he hasn't killed anyone, and, yes, he is a PI prodigy."

"Look, auntie, why don't you sit down on the floor beside that dreadful settee you have and pipe down?" Mechanix gave Bea some twine and a roll of gray duct tape and ordered her to restrain Beryl's hands, stifle her vocal cords, and tie her tightly to one of the wooden legs.

Bea concurred, not wanting to upset Mechanix to the point of getting the row home and its residents torched.

"Okay, Mrs. Tend—"

"We're not married yet."

"Regardless, if you don't cooperate, you may never get hitched. The two of us are going for a short ride in a nice big black stretch limousine to retrieve your Mr. Tender. Kind of like Timmy and Bea going on a prom date with a dangerously impulsive chaperone. You drive." Mechanix rearranged his backpack and gently pushed the flamethrower hose into the curve just above Bea's lower back. "Off to see the PI wizard!"

CHAPTER 29

Morris Mechanix's House
Monday, 12:45 p.m. EST

The big Lincoln Continental was pulling up in front of the brick row home of the person that was sitting in the car's extreme back seat, Morris Mechanix. The glass partition that separated the driver from the passenger, usually an individual of a position a few steps up the financial ladder than the vehicle's operator, was in the down position.

Private Eye Tender was on the porch already expecting this kind of scenario. He had brought, just in case, his pearl-handled Colt .45, which had been given to him as a gift from his former fifth-grade teacher, long ago advanced to the principal's position—well-deserved. He put his left hand inside his jacket onto the firearm butt, forefinger on the side of the trigger—barrel hidden by the holster. He was prepared for extreme foul play.

Then the passenger's front window of the stretch came down, and Tender saw something he couldn't believe: his precious Bea sitting behind the steering wheel. Tender's hand immediately left the revolver.

"Timster, can you come here?"

"Tell him to drop his gun," a voice from the backseat demanded.

"Better leave the Colt there; Mechanix's got the drop on me."

"With what? The .22 has been secured," Tender said.

The back window came down and the flamethrower made its exodus. "Will this convince you, Tenderfoot?"

Tender quickly emptied the bullets to prevent any unforseen accident if someone found the firearm. The .45 entered a bush next to the walkway that led to the porch. "What are you doing with my girl—"

"Don't worry, I won't hurt her—that is if you cooperate and hop in the back. We need to take a ride and chat."

Tender performed as requested.

"Okay, Mrs. Tender, head toward the Parkway and point the wheels in the direction of DC, got it?"

"Yes, I got it assh—"

"Whoa! Tender, she's spunkier than a pissed-off poodle—sure you can handle that, huh?"

"What do you want to talk about?"

"I presume that you found everything needed to have me arrested for the Jake Venom and King Bench killings?"

"You can carve that in stone; the evidence is on its way to Central District One, Baltimore PD." It may still be sitting in a nice, neat pile on the green love seat, but Mechanix didn't need that information. "One thing: where are the snakes that were in the aquarium?"

"What makes you think I didn't have some tropical fish in there named Goldie or Hi-Ho Silver?"

"Because freshwater fish need, at the very least, *freshwater*, not wood chips. And I don't think they eat dead rats."

"Good, Tender. How'd you know that?"

"I read."

"Well, I set the cobras free in the woods, a reptile should be in its natural habitat, don't you think?"

"Then you should have mailed them to Africa and Asia," Bea E. responded.

"You know your snakes," Mechanix said.

"I read too. You let those deadly snakes loose where they might strike some innocent passer-by, you are an imbec—"

"Look, spitting vinegar only goes so far. If you don't pipe down, I'm going to close the partition, or maybe torch that lovely, long dark hair of yours. Just kidding, Tender, about that last part—she has to drive right now."

"You touch a strand of her hair—"

"Right, you're a tough guy, I know."

"You sound a little nervous, just like you did each time you were lying to me," Tender said.

"Doesn't matter now, does it? I admit it: I snuffed Jake Venom and King Bench but not the other two—what were their names?"

"Fredric Price and Vincent March," Bea chimed in.

"She's a regular Della Street, isn't she?"

Tender said, "She's the best, and if you hurt her in any way, you'll regret it the rest of your low life."

"I truly believe that but right now I've got the upper hand, and I'm dealing the cards, so sit there and listen. And you need to take a right here, Mrs. Tender; it's a shortcut."

Bea quickly swung the wheel around clockwise, jerking both the rear passengers from their present positions.

"Lady, take it easy; this isn't the Daytona 500," Mechanix said. "There's no rush!"

Tender said, "I know why you killed Jake Venom. I figured it out when I tested that old Remington typewriter of yours."

"Okay, smart guy, go ahead."

"When I was browsing around Jake's office, I came upon a rough draft of *Tender Nightmare.* Closer scrutiny revealed a curious thing." Tender and Mechanix both shifted in their seats to get more comfortable. "All the words where an *O* should have been were actually *Q*s. That's the same thing your typewriter does with the shift key on. Therefore, it follows you are the one who wrote that book, not Venom. Am I correct?"

"Timster, are you serious, this bonehead is a writer?"

Mechanix clapped three times loudly. "Congratulations, Sherlock, you got it."

"My only question there is, Why did you type the whole manuscript in capital letters?"

"Ever hear the expression 'See your name in lights? That was my version, my writing stood out more, and I began to like the *Q*s—I enjoy reading *my* writing."

Bea added, "So how did Jake Venom get the credit?"

"And the money! The son-of-a—that's why I reacted the way I did when your auntie mentioned the *innocent* victims."

"Why'd you quit going for your English degree at the University of Maine?" Tender said.

"You've done your homework. I'm impressed."

"With a little help from a friend," Bea said.

"I dropped out because the professors didn't seem to know as much as I did."

"Only problem is it got you drafted, right?"

"Right. That's when the real troubles started, but that story comes later—back to that snake, Venom. You got the symbolism; I was proud of that."

"Got it," Tender mumbled. "Go on. By the way, what did you do with the rough draft and the yellow ski mask after you knocked me out? I didn't see them in your place."

"Safe in a safety deposit box at Maryland National Bank. Anyway, I had done a lot of charters for Venom and his snobby friends, and I knew the first time I saw him that he had a coke problem."

"Rawness under his nose, right?"

"And his upper lip was always redder than the lights in front of a redlight district."

"Or your '59 GMC converted into a limousine."

"How'd you know that?"

"You cut me off once. I realized it was you after I trailed you from your agency office to your real living quarters. And I have a nice picture of the truck."

"I wanted to ask you about that. I picked up your car right away and then lost you on Orleans."

"That was the friend Bea alluded to before; he was driving my 'stang, and I grabbed your trail using his car."

"Timster's good, isn't he, huh?" Bea said tensely.

Tender had just realized, after hearing his girl utter "huh," that he hadn't used the expression himself in this whole conversation. Maybe he could finally lose it. "So you became Jake's supplier, right?" he continued.

"Ah! the King Bench connection," Bea E. noted.

"King wasn't a dealer, just a runner; he knew how to get the stuff to where it needed to go. One day when I was waiting for the famous horror writer inside one of his favorite cat houses on the Block, I came up with an idea: I'd approach him with a proposition that I could keep him heavy into the blow, or get him some in a more concentrated pellet form that he could smoke through some special gear, which King also had access to. That way he could lay off his nose, and he wouldn't have to worry about trying to get the stuff himself."

"And his part of the bargain would be to help you get your book published, right? Let me ask you another thing that I was curious about: why did the rough draft have the initials J. V. in the byline?" Tender said.

"My pseudonym is John Victor; I started using it when I lost some limo business. It's not important. What is important is that the mutant of terror material stole my manuscript and published it as his own.

"The favor was returned after I eighty-sixed him; I copped his script called *The Godfather of Bane*. But when I got through reading it, I understood why he felt he had to steal mine. It was trash. Makes me wonder how he could have written any of the others that he sold so many copies."

"Could not have been any worse than *The Fascist Dean*," Tender said. "What did you do with *The Godfather of Bane*?"

"After I attempted to copy it and realized what a piece of crap it was, I set it on fire. No way I'd send that anywhere with my name on it, having publishers, editors, or agents think I penned that garbage."

"*You were a bad boy it was deserved* highlighted in the Webster's was clever," Tender said, thinking it a good idea to keep his and Bea's captor off-balance with praise and not upset him into firing up his weapon of choice.

"Yes, ingenious, I thought."

"Of course, according to you, there must've been a copycat killer, using your creation of highlighting words—only in a Doubleday Dictionary," Bea said.

"Which proves, at least to me, that I couldn't have done in the other two because of already expending good money on enough Webster's to do all the jobs. I don't spend frivolously."

"Plus, I believe you're obsessed with doing things in an identical pattern, right?" Tender said, using his skills learned during his minor in psychology at Fresno State.

"Do you know that you're saying 'right' quite a bit?" Mechanix observed. "I prefer the 'huh' better."

"I didn't notice. I'll have to work on that."

"Good. But, you're correct: I do have that compulsion."

"Hence, *A double-cross gets what it deserves* for King Bench," Bea added. "What does that mean? By the way, are you a Virgo? If I didn't know that Timster had been born under the sign of the bull, I would've bet—something he does too often—that he was a Virgo for sure. He has that same habit."

Tender replied, "I'm gonna quit, Bea. I'm trying. And can we dispense with the astrology references?"

Mechanix shifted the flamethrower. "Hey! I feel like a family counselor here. I'm on stage here. Can I continue, please?"

"Before you explain," Tender said, "let me guess the reason for the paperback version of the Webster's."

"Fire away."

"Easy: Jake was a famous author, and King was a punk outlaw."

"You're on the right track with the symbolic reference, but your reason isn't dead-on; I chose the different forms according to the degree of injustice shown to me."

"And you feel that what you did to them balances the ledger?" Tender said.

"You got it."

Tender felt, and knew Bea would agree, that this guy's rationale was diseased—and he needed serious help. But the push for more information had to continue, so verbal judgment was withheld for the time being. He didn't want Mechanix's recent phrase, *fire away*, to become a reality.

"So why King, huh?" Bea E. asked.

"As the dictionary stated, he double-crossed me. He got what he deserved."

"Must've had something to do with Jake's Jaguar, right? Baltimore PD found his fingerprints all over it," Tender said.

"You're amazing, PI. That's it. King helped me out once; one thing he wasn't was a rat, he—"

"No, he was a mouse. You are the rat!" Bea pushed that statement in easier than a needle entering an overused vein.

"Tender, you'd better tell her to quit interrupting."

"She's got a mind of her own. Get used to it."

"If I can continue? King did me a favor once, and I knew he was short of funds—usually was. I decided to let him help me, and I'd pay him more than he was getting from his drug runs."

Tender knew the dishonorable Vietnam favor Mechanix was talking about but kept it to himself, for now. "Did you think you were going to get rich off Venom's latest story?"

"Possibly. He did have a rep, continued through my work. But selling that emerald green '68 XJ 6 of his—a fine piece of machinery—would have brought a nice price; I have connections."

"Overseas shipper?" Tender said.

"You got it. Turns out that good ole King tried to peddle it to one of his local chop shop buddies, take the money, and run. He didn't know that I swung a lot of business to Perry at Mason Travel, which was where Bench purchased a one-way ticket to New York City, thinking he could get lost in the crowd."

"So honorable," Bea said sarcastically.

"King also didn't realize that my overseas guy knew his chop shop guy. I guess after the King Bench rubout, nobody wanted anything to do with the Jaguar."

"After recruiting his services, how did you use Mr. Bench?" Tender said.

"The Monday morning of his later retribution, Venom called and wanted me to take him to the post office and then to the Freedom Inn. It was perfect—he had already left a note for his wife about his whereabouts. I could tell by the slurring of his speech that he was already somewhat stoned. I could make out that he said Mrs. Venom had gone to the Milhous Salon on Pennsylvania Avenue and would be there most of the day. I'd been waiting for the perfect opportunity, and this was it. I took my Sudanese Cobra, the .22, two pairs of surgical gloves, my best Webster's, and King. Destination: the house on Silverbirch. And as I suspected, Jake could barely stand up. It made things too easy. I wanted him to understand more than he was able to. Oh, well. King had to hot-wire the Jag because we couldn't find the key."

Tender interrupted. "The keys were behind the dollar bill on the wall. And I hate to rub this in, but it was the first skin he dishonestly pocketed on your *Tender Nightmare*."

"Maybe he left it to me in his will," Mechanix said with a smirk.

The mention of the will made Tender think of Mrs. Venom and the outrageous monies she had garnered.

"If you had given King surgical gloves, how did his fingerprints end up on the Jag?"

"Must've thrown them away. King wasn't too smart. I told him to hide the car until things cooled down; instead, he tried to pull the double-cross. Bad move."

"His dumbest move was getting involved with you," Bea added.

"I don't like to be crossed."

"Tell me about Vietnam," Tender said.

"What about it? It's a crappy war, and we should've never gotten into it—thank you, good ole number thirty-six."

"You may be right, but I'm talking about your relationship with King Bench in Nam. Weren't you in the same outfit?"

"You're a regular encyclopedia of insignificant information."

"Yea, just like your Webster's!" Bea said.

"Funny," Mechanix stated.

"And the favor you mentioned earlier was that Bench didn't give you up in the incident with the Asian bar owner that you two beat up—like real soldiers. Otherwise, you might've been dishonorably discharged too and end up maybe sharing King's apartment and lifestyle. Nice gratitude on your part."

"Man, the war sucks. Obviously, you didn't have to go, or you'd know that. Things happened, and you never knew who was on whose side, who was gonna befriend you and then stab you in the back."

Tender added, "Apparently, the military tribunal at King's court-martial didn't agree with your assessment in 'the case of the bar owner beating,' right?"

"Timster, you have to stop saying 'right,' huh?"

"Bea, you have to stop saying 'huh,' right? Okay, let's both go cold turkey. Boom! Done."

"Man, you two are too much."

"Sorry," Tender said. "Continue."

"There's nothing much more to say. The command decided to make me a Mr. Zippo—you know what that is?"

Tender responded, "The flamethrower. Why you?"

"I guess because I was always talking about being fascinated with the awesome power of the fire surrounding the huts that always seemed to be burning. When they first gave me the weapon, I could feel in my hands the remarkable power that seemed to ooze out of it. I felt invincible. But …"

"But what?" Bea asked. She and Tender were sitting still but not unaware of their dangerous situation. They felt Mechanix could go off at any moment.

"The initial time I used the flamethrower, the reaction was the opposite. I flamed a VC and watched his body go from life and yellowish to death and crispy black. There was steam rising from the form, which at that point was all that it was." For a moment, Mechanix put his head down as if in shame. "After that scene, I started using drugs to cope—regular marijuana first, then a sinsemilla for a stronger high, and finally LSD, which continued in Haight-Ashbury.

"I made an exception and used the acid when I did Venom and Bench. In those trips, they were each the enemy—Lucifer, the fallen angel. Old Serpent," Mechanix said.

"The snakes as a murder weapon," Tender said.

"Right, huh," Mechanix said. "And the .22 to bring home a point. I never used a flamethrower after that."

At that instant, Tender got a sensation that Mechanix might be giving up to his burdens.

Bea Hopkins didn't have the same reaction. She flipped her dark hair back from the right side of her head, a prearranged signal that she and Tender had developed for predicaments such as the present one. It meant something was going to happen.

Bea jammed her right foot on the limousine's brake pedal, Mechanix lunged forward, and Tender held the door handle. Bea then hit the accelerator, and Mechanix flew back.

Tender had caught the signal and then used a skill he had learned in his Lakehood High days in Saint Petersburg: a powerful left jab landed square on Mechanix's right chin that would have made the Greatest, Muhammad Ali, proud.

Mechanix was out instantly. The flamethrower fell passively to the expensively carpeted floor.

The temporary chauffeur, Bea E. Hopkins, turned the Lincoln Continental around and headed toward the downtown Baltimore Police Department.

CHAPTER 30

Monday, 3:00 p.m. EST
Central District 1
Baltimore Police Department

After getting the news about Mechanix's capture, Lieutenant Ripken Omaha left the Lord Baltimore Hotel to meet his two friends, Tim Tender and Bea E. Hopkins, at the police station. When he arrived, he found that Sergeant Small and Detective Broadly had obtained taped confessions from Vicki Venom and Pasta E. Fagioli, his much shorter than hers. Sworn statements were transcribed and signed.

After Mechanix was processed, booked and carted away, Tender wanted to chat with Vicki Venom. Unfortunately, after meeting with Omaha, Tender discovered that she was done and refused to talk to anyone else. So, Tender and Omaha met with Small and Broadly to get the full story. Sergeant Small had handled all the questioning of Mrs. Venom—Detective Broadly had been given the unenviable task of trying to squeeze out more information than the limited amount Fagioli was willing to lay down.

A uniform officer and Bea E. went to free Aunt Beryl.

The law-seeking quadruplet sat around one of the suspect interview tables, and after Sergeant Small engaged the rewind button, they waited. The ribbon reached the beginning of Vicki's *fessing-up*, and Small pushed the start symbol, fast-forwarded past the date, participants, etc. The foursome sat and listened.

"Go ahead, Mrs. Venom, the tape is running."

"I, Vicki Venom, am confessing to conspiring to kill my husband, Jake Venom. The persons whom I conspired with are the following: Vincent March, Aldo Linguine, Pasta E. Fagioli, and Don Jonah Vermicelli. Unfortunately, someone else got to him before we could; therefore, we are not responsible for his death. And I did devise a plan with the latter three Italian food names mentioned above, and Vincent March, to have—"

"Please mention the names, Mrs. Venom, and start from the beginning of the sentence."

"I also devised a plan with Aldo Linguine, Pasta E. Fagioli, Don Jonah Vermicelli, and Vincent March to eliminate Fredric Price. The plan was carried out perfectly. The original idea to eliminate Fredric Price was proposed by Vincent March."

"Why would Mr. March want to kill his senior editor?"

"As the Doubleday Dictionary stated, he was blackmailing Vincent because he found out that Jake didn't write *Tender Nightmare*, and he also knew that we were having an affair and planning to permanently eliminate my dear-departed husband."

"We?"

"Vincent and I."

"Vincent?"

"Yes, yes, Vincent March. Look, I knew my husband humped whores, but for some reason, he didn't think I knew, so I used it to my advantage. He would always claim how much he loved me. I had him increase his life insurance so I could live the way I had become accustomed to after marrying a rich man. It was his own fault. When we got married, we were very happy; he lavished me with jewels, furs, exotic vacations, fancy dinners, and Broadway shows—all the things that I had never experienced before meeting him. Well, the relationship started going sour. He started playing around and doing drugs. Then his writing started to suffer, which is why he decided to steal the manuscript written by Morris Mechanix. If you want a suspect for Jake's murder, I would think that Mr. Mechanix had a real good motive, considering the kind of money that book made.

"I knew that I could use my feminine charms—I noticed you glimpsing at my legs—to convince Vincent March to bargain with me to get rid of Jake, who made the mistake of cheating on the wrong woman. Of course, he must've committed an even bigger betrayal to whoever killed him.

"What was Mr. March supposed to get out of the bargain?"

"For me to marry him, honeymoon in Athens—"

"Georgia?"

"Ha-ha. Athens, Greece."

"What's so funny?"

"Oh, I'm not snickering at you. It's just that Mr. March and I had kind of that same exchange."

"Continue please, Mrs. Venom."

"Along with becoming Mrs. March, which would never have happened, he wanted me—with my inheritance and insurance money—to help him save his faltering company, which began to go down about the same time Jake started to snort cocaine. I figured Jake had put Premature Burial Publishing on the map, but I wasn't going to spend my hard-earned money on keeping it there. Vincent March was a buffoon, hence the harlequin reference for his Doubleday Dictionary.

"I conspired with Pasta E. Fagioli, Aldo Linguine, and Don Jonah Vermicelli to have Vincent March bumped off."

"Obviously, in Fredric Price's and Vincent March's murders, you were trying to make it look like Jake's killer committed theirs too. So why not use a Webster's?"

"Because they were all gone; someone had bought all of them. I didn't have time to wait for the reorders. And I never knew about the snake venom."

"How did you come to engage the three Sicilians?"

"They came to the house one day to see Jake. They wanted him to advise them on what to do about a manuscript that the oldest one had written. They claimed that Mario Puzo had stolen their idea for *The Godfather*. Jake wouldn't help them because he thought it was a ridiculous notion. But they asked him if he wouldn't mind having his picture taken with them. They thought being seen with him might help their cause. He reluctantly agreed. I took the snapshot, as Jake requested. Before they left, they said that they were staying at the Lord Baltimore Hotel in room 1939, if he changed his mind."

"That still doesn't answer my question."

Be patient; I'm getting to it. I could see that the Sicilians were infuriated with Jake, so, I went to their hotel, knowing the financial situation that I would be in after Jake died, and 'made them an offer they couldn't refuse.' They said that was Puzo's line, not Vermicelli's. I set the hit for the Monday while I would be at Milhous Salon for my monthly rejuvenation."

"Your alibi, the Mane Magician."

"Right, Sergeant. Monday was one of Jake's favorite days to write—some superstition about a 'new week, new motivation' babble he would quote. Anyway, I knew he'd be home all day. I made sure to leave the front door open when I left".

"You contend that when Fagioli, Linguine, and Don Vermicelli, aka the Sicilians, arrived to carry out the contract, your husband was gone."

"Correct. And when I read the note, I figured it was true. So, I delayed the hit for the time being."

"What did you do next, Mrs. Venom?"

I waited until Wednesday, but Jake never showed, so I hired Tim Tender, the private eye, to locate him. And then Thursday he was found dead. I contacted Mr. Linguine to see if they had fulfilled the contract, and he assured me that they had nothing to do with it. But they agreed to continue the contract and garner their payment in any way I chose. The wheels started turning, and they completed their task via Fredric Price. Vincent said it was perfect, and our alibis for Price's snuffing were confirmed—his by Hesta Perrine, the secretary at Premature Burial Publishing. Mine was verified by Thelma, Vincent's housekeeper."

"Did you show March a little leg?"

Oh, much more than that, Sergeant".

"First, if the Sicilians brought closure to the contract, why did Pasta E. Fagioli kill Vincent March? Second, why were you trying to leave the country with him? Third, why was March in room 1939 at the Lord Baltimore Hotel when he was killed?"

"I sent Vincent there, telling him that I had lost an earring in the room at the first meeting with the Sicilians. If found by you or your colleagues, it would not have been good. It was Vincent's idea to use Price's name on the hotel register—kind of tacky, I thought. One thing I didn't perceive in my plans was that I would fall in love with Pasta E.—and vice versa. He did Vincent March free of charge, to show his undying love for moi."

"Mrs. Venom, you know Italian, or is that French?"

Right. The Big Pasta and I thought by lying low for a couple of days before leaving the country, we could escape easier than dripping olive oil into a frying pan. Unfortunately, we were out to lunch."

The tape recorder shut off.

"There you have it," Sergeant Small said.

"Doesn't sound like much remorse is evident," Tender said. "Too cool, calculating."

"Sounds conclusive, though," Lieutenant Omaha added.

"Pasta Fagioli's confession, though not quite as clear, corroborates her story," Detective Broadly added to the conversation. "What's the next step?"

"Extradition proceedings!" the remaining trio of justice-seekers expressed in harmony.

EPILOGUE

Sunday, December 26, 1970
Baltimore, Maryland

Tender advised, "Having allowed enough time for all the recent, dreadful events to gain some distance from tenseness to tranquility of the Baltimore faithful, these are the facts."

Life expectancy in this year of our Lord is 71.1 years. Some of the players listed below did not or may not reach that level:

Morris Mechanix's lawyer had gained him an insanity plea in the deaths of Jake Venom and King Bench. Mechanix would be spending the rest of his days in, ironically, the mental institution generally acclaimed to be the best in the country, Saint Sid's Sanitarium of Saint Petersburg, Florida.

The co-conspirators, Vicki Venom and Aldo Linguine, would be doing life stretches in federal prison.

Pasta E. Fagioli, the actual trigger man in both the killings of Fredric Price and Vincent March, would be wasting away on death row on the green mile.

Don Jonah Vermicelli would not be staying at any correctional facility, or any institution for that matter. The don died on the extradition plane flying from London to Baltimore, not getting his wish to expire in the old country.

The stolen manuscript, *Tender Nightmare*, was retrieved from the safety deposit box at Maryland National Bank. Proper credit was given to an extremely troubled man.

The marvelous *Baltimore Sun Newspaper* reported about one exciting event on the Charmed City's social calendar: the marriage ceremony and reception of Bea E. Hopkins and Tim Tender.

With the NFL Colts recently victorious in the Super Bowl and Lt. Omaha being a city employee, Memorial Stadium was gratefully, and at no charge, provided for the nuptials. The infield was chalked as if an Orioles' baseball match was about to take place, complete with left and right batter's boxes, along with the third and first baselines. Also, the pews were overlapping the dual white stripes.

The Colt footballers were seated on the groom's side (third base) along with his family and friends; the bride's kin and the Oriole baseballers were squeezed into the remaining church benches (first base area).

The vows were spoken beside home plate, Bea in the right batter's square and Tim in the left box. Todd, Tender's four-minute-older twin, was standing as best man, and Bea's best friend, Wendy, also up from Saint Petersburg and a favorite of the fabulous Beach Boys, filled the maid of honor spot. Ushers included the now promoted Captain Ripken "Rip" Omaha, Vincent Price, Ernest Borgnine, and Mario Puzo. Bridesmaids in attendance were Elizabeth Taylor, Dorothy Lamour, and the identical twins Esther Pauline Friedman Lederer and Pauline Esther Friedman Phillips, better known as Ann Landers and Abigail Van Buren. The two, having been married in a double-hitching service in 1939, were able to give Bea some valuable marital advice.

Tender also had in his portion of the vows, advanced by his future wife, the promise to quit gambling cold gobbler.

A friend of Bea's family, Reverend Cox, said, "I now pronounce you man and wife. May I present Mr. and Mrs. Tim Tender."

It was a wonderful wedding, as described on the front page of the *Sun*.

After the marvelous reception, and a dinner party floating at Sunset on the Chesapeake Bay, the newlyweds traveled not on a cruise but to a wonderful place just the same: the Chesapeake Wood Duck Inn on Tilghman Island, Maryland.

Tender provided directions in the Baltimore Sun, if you want to visit this beautiful property: From Route 50 East, take Route 322 to Route 33. Follow Route 33 through St. Michaels to Tilghman Island. Once over the drawbridge, turn left on Gibsontown Road. The inn sits directly on the right of Dogwood Harbor.

PI Tender strongly requested that you shelve your visit to the Wood Duck until the Tenders have vacated for the second part of their honeymoon at the fabulous Hollander Hotel, built-in 1933, just as Prohibition ended, still with the original facade reminiscent of the Bonnie and Clyde era. It also resides in Tender's home state, Florida.

There, Tim and Bea Tender, the seventies version of Dashiell Hammett's detective team of the thirties, Nick and Nora Charles, would await their next challenge.

The End